CHICAGO PI'

☑ **W9-BTD-456**

R030b1 ᒧᒪ᠐ᒪ᠐

Cut from the same cloth, they'd either kill each other or love each other like no other. Either way, they were doomed.

Cissy slid out the car door. "You'll let me know if you get anything from Eddie."

"What are we? Partners now?"

"That's right. Call me." She slammed the door and walked to the motel office, giving Nick her best backside show.

If she were sixteen again, and he was seventeen, he would gun the engine and peel out. But she wasn't sixteen. He wasn't seventeen. She was thirty-two with a missing mother and sister and only a month of severance between her and the streets. He was thirty-three, a detective who had seen human depravity in all its many incarnations. Still, she'd bet her last year of decent dividends that as he eased the unmarked vehicle into traffic and pulled smoothly away, he was smiling. Just like her.

NORTH AUSTIN BRANCH
5724 W. NORTH AVE.
CHICAGO, IL 60639

Dear Harlequin Intrigue Reader,

Take a very well-deserved break from Thanksgiving preparations and rejuvenate yourself with Harlequin Intrigue's tempting offerings this month!

To start off the festivities, Harper Allen brings you *Covert Cowboy*—the next riveting installment of COLORADO CONFIDENTIAL. Watch the sparks fly when a Native American secret agent teams up with the headstrong mother of his unborn child to catch a slippery criminal. Looking to live on the edge? Then enter the dark and somber HEARTSKEEP estate—with caution!—when Dani Sinclair brings you *The Second Sister*—the next book in her gothic trilogy.

The thrills don't stop there! *His Mysterious Ways* pairs a ruthless mercenary with a secretive seductress as they ward off evil forces. Don't miss this new series in Amanda Stevens's extraordinary QUANTUM MEN books. Join Mallory Kane for an action-packed story about a heroine who must turn to a tough-hearted FBI operative when she's targeted by a stalker in *Bodyguard/Husband*.

A homecoming unveils a deadly conspiracy in *Unmarked Man* by Darlene Scalera—the latest offering in our new theme promotion BACHELORS AT LARGE. And finally this month, 'tis the season for some spine-tingling suspense in *The Christmas Target* by Charlotte Douglas when a sexy cowboy cop must ride to the rescue as a twisted Santa sets his sights on a beautiful businesswoman.

So gather your loved ones all around and warm up by the fire with some steamy romantic suspense!

Enjoy,

Denise O'Sullivan
Senior Editor
Harlequin Intrigue

UNMARKED MAN

DARLENE SCALERA

NORTH AUSTIN BRANCH
5724 W. NORTH AVE.
CHICAGO, IL 60639

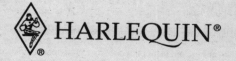

HARLEQUIN®

TORONTO • NEW YORK • LONDON
AMSTERDAM • PARIS • SYDNEY • HAMBURG
STOCKHOLM • ATHENS • TOKYO • MILAN • MADRID
PRAGUE • WARSAW • BUDAPEST • AUCKLAND

If you purchased this book without a cover you should be aware
that this book is stolen property. It was reported as "unsold and
destroyed" to the publisher, and neither the author nor the
publisher has received any payment for this "stripped book."

R03061 21815

ISBN 0-373-22739-6

UNMARKED MAN

Copyright © 2003 by Darlene Scalera.

All rights reserved. Except for use in any review, the reproduction or
utilization of this work in whole or in part in any form by any electronic,
mechanical or other means, now known or hereafter invented, including
xerography, photocopying and recording, or in any information storage
or retrieval system, is forbidden without the written permission of the
publisher, Harlequin Enterprises Limited, 225 Duncan Mill Road,
Don Mills, Ontario, Canada M3B 3K9.

All characters in this book have no existence outside the imagination of
the author and have no relation whatsoever to anyone bearing the same
name or names. They are not even distantly inspired by any individual
known or unknown to the author, and all incidents are pure invention.

This edition published by arrangement with Harlequin Books S.A.

® and TM are trademarks of the publisher. Trademarks indicated with
® are registered in the United States Patent and Trademark Office, the
Canadian Trade Marks Office and in other countries.

Visit us at www.eHarlequin.com

Printed in U.S.A.

ABOUT THE AUTHOR

Darlene Scalera is a native New Yorker who graduated magna cum laude from Syracuse University with a degree in public communications. She worked in a variety of fields, including telecommunications and public relations, before devoting herself full-time to romance fiction writing. She was instrumental in forming the Saratoga, New York, chapter of Romance Writers of America and is a frequent speaker on romance writing at local schools, libraries, writing groups and women's organizations. She currently lives happily ever after in upstate New York with her husband, Jim, and their two children, J.J. and Ariana. You can write to Darlene at P.O. Box 217, Niverville, NY 12130.

Books by Darlene Scalera

HARLEQUIN INTRIGUE
739—UNMARKED MAN

HARLEQUIN AMERICAN ROMANCE
762—A MAN FOR MEGAN
807—MAN IN A MILLION
819—THE COWBOY AND THE COUNTESS
861—PRESCRIPTION FOR SEDUCTION
896—BORN OF THE BLUEGRASS
923—HELP WANTED: HUSBAND?
967—MAY THE BEST MAN WED

Don't miss any of our special offers. Write to us at the following address for information on our newest releases.

Harlequin Reader Service
U.S.: 3010 Walden Ave., P.O. Box 1325, Buffalo, NY 14269
Canadian: P.O. Box 609, Fort Erie, Ont. L2A 5X3

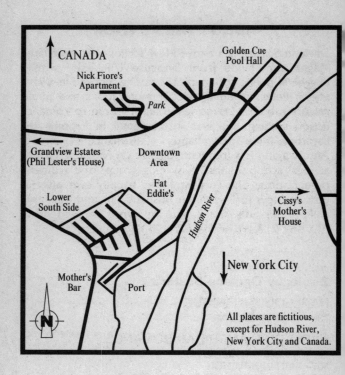

CANADA

Nick Fiore's
Apartment

Park

Golden Cue
Pool Hall

Grandview Estates
(Phil Lester's House)

Downtown
Area

Fat
Eddie's

Hudson River

Cissy's
Mother's
House

Lower
South Side

New York City

Mother's
Bar

Port

N

All places are fictitious,
except for Hudson River,
New York City and Canada.

CAST OF CHARACTERS

Cissy Spagnola—The disappearance of her mother and sister have pushed her back into the arms of her first love, a man who could ruin Cissy faster than a cheap bikini wax.

Nick Fiore—Bad boy turned cop, he now protects the same mean streets he once ruled. It's his duty—and desire—to stay as close as possible to Cissy.

Fat Eddie Spagnola—No one believes the violent drunk when he claims his wife stole some cash and left him in the middle of the night—least of all his stepdaughter.

Louise Spagnola—She believed in the sacraments of her religion…and she loved her red 1950s Thunderbird. What would make her suddenly abandon them both?

JoJo Spagnola—Cissy's little sister had a habit of falling for the wrong kind of man. But would this last man be the end of her?

Tommy Marcus—He has the face of a padre and the connections of a politician. Cissy hopes his help will lead her to her mother and sister.

Philip Lester—The unassuming suburban tax clerk has a black Harley and friends like "Stevie the Sledgehammer."

The Lords—An FBI sweep broke this gang up years ago, but they're back to reclaim their South Side stronghold.

Chapter One

The streets were narrower than Cissy Spagnola's memory. Front yards were a stoop flush to cement. Later, after the day's high heat, fat old ladies would set up chairs on the sidewalks to scream at each other in Italian.

The station house was a dung-colored square with dirty windows. The neglect continued inside with scarred chairs, slow-turning ceiling fans, files stacked high and carelessly.

Cissy moved to the front desk. "I want to file a missing person's report," she told the woman behind the brown desk.

The woman didn't look up. "Child or adult?"

"Adult."

"Mentally disabled?"

"No," Cissy told the woman's crown in need of a touch up.

"Physically disabled? In need of medication?"

"No."

"Possible victim of foul play?"

"Bingo." Cissy had never perfected the art of making friends.

The woman's head snapped up. Her mascara had already begun to melt. "Gruber," she yelled, her eyes shish-kebabing Cissy. "Possible missing." She jerked her head toward the back, her sprayed bouffant solid. "Third desk on the right."

Cissy was almost to the waiting Gruber with the keen, beady gaze when she heard her name spat as a question. She yanked her head around to find herself chest to rib cage with Nick Fiore. He was bigger than she liked to remember and solid as the brick walls she'd been running into her whole life. He sported the shaved hairstyle popular among cops, sports figures and skinheads, the white of his scalp suggesting an innocence Cissy knew he'd never known in his thirty-three years. The planes of his face were steeper, the line of his mouth as hard as when she had first pressed her own to it.

She reined herself in while he checked out her two-hundred-dollar haircut, the designer clothes, the air of success and confidence she'd struggled for since she was ten. Only she knew the third-rate brokerage firm where she'd worked had gone bust, her stock portfolio was in the crapper along with her ex-customers' and her personal financial strategy of making no more than 'the monthly minimum required' was a hint as to why she should never have stepped onto Wall Street in the first place.

But she forgot all that as her gaze fell to where it

shouldn't have, and she caught the badge low on her old lover's belt loops.

"Son of a bitch," she said to life in general, more specifically to the unwelcome hum in her limbs gaining power.

The hard lines of Nick's face cracked with a one-sided smirk. "Can take the girl out of the neighborhood but can't take the neighborhood out of the girl?"

Before she had a chance to redeem herself with a more tasteful response, the man who'd taken her virginity on a studio couch with bad springs turned to his fellow officer. "I've got this one." With the same power he'd used to claim her maidenhood, Cissy was led to a cubicle with fake oak walls.

"Have a seat." He indicated the worn chair by the desk. She thought of bad springs.

She tried for an elegant lift of her head. "Are you sure it's ethical for you to handle this report, considering our past?" Much better than her initial discharge.

He propped one muscled hip on the desk's corner and smiled down at her.

His eyes alone could make a woman say yes.

She tightened her mouth, tightened her limbs. "Don't try and weasel out of it by telling me you don't remember."

"I remember."

His tone, even more than his honesty, told her the man he'd become. She shot him a smile. After all, she had been as eager as he. Last virgin on the block had held no honor in her neighborhood. Nor any pleasure for a curious teenager whose closest run-in with titillation had been when she confused which orifice between her legs should be plugged with a tampon.

"Nick Fiore. A cop. Damn." She plopped down in the chair. A spring impaled her.

He cocked his head, gave her another good, long once-over. "Stockbroker?" he said as if it were a guess.

Her eyes narrowed. "You're good but you're not that good."

He chuckled, the sound hitting her square in the gut. "You've got a ripped up stock order ticket stuck on a wad of gum on the bottom of your shoe."

So much for aplomb. He was right. She stunk of the neighborhood.

"My mother might have mentioned it, too."

He could have gotten away without telling her that and impressed her big time. He hadn't.

"More than once," he added in a way that said his mother had harangued him daily.

Cissy suddenly adored Mrs. Fiore. "How is your mother?"

"Moved to Coco Beach two years ago with a guy with Elvis hair."

Knocks on the door of the yellow rowhouse with the brown roof at 2:00 a.m., Cissy and her sister on the stoop in their pajamas. The door would open to Mrs. Fiore, cigarette in hand, pink tape across her bangs and the spitcurls in front of her ears. Some-

*times Cissy's mother had still been bleeding, always
starting to swell. Once there'd been cracked ribs...*

He studied her, the pain of his own past no less
than her own. "She was right. You did okay, Cissy,
for a skinny, flat-chested runt from the neighborhood."

"I wasn't too skinny for you one night." But already her voice was softening. Even if he had broken
her heart, she'd happily handed it to him. And Nick's
mother had been a good friend to Louisa Vitelli and
her two girls. Not that Mrs. Fiore had ever been able
to convince Cissy's mother to leave her second husband. Mrs. Fiore's own marriage had ended after her
thirteen-year-old son had tried one Saturday night to
protect her from her drunken husband. It'd taken
twelve years and Nick's two-week hospital stay. So
Mrs. Fiore understood what didn't seem understand-
able, and with a cloud of smoke and hot pink curls,
opened her door to Cissy and her sister and mother
any time day or night. Even knowing after one or two
days, an apology and the promise it would never happen again, and Louisa would go home to Eddie.

"You didn't do so bad yourself, Fiore."

He smiled. The hum inside her swelled.

"For a lying skunk."

His expression showed no offense. "I didn't lie,
Cissy. And you aren't stuck in a three-story walk-up
with sagging boobs and a couple of kids on a cop's
salary."

"Hell, no."

He smiled wider. "Then what are you pissed at me for?"

She attempted indignation. "You could have at least called and given me the chance to turn you down."

"I wasn't that nice a guy."

"You weren't a nice guy at all."

"I'm still not a nice guy."

Cissy heard the warning and appreciated it.

"So, what brings you back down memory lane?"

"My mother. I'm afraid something's happened to her. She's missing."

"Missing?" He became all cop now. Again Cissy saw the man he had become.

"I called her last night. My sister had left a message on my machine yesterday to call her. She sounded a bit hysterical, but then again, that's not unusual for Jo Jo. She seems to thrive on high drama. I called the last number I had for her, but it'd been disconnected. That's also not unusual for Jo Jo. So I called my mother to see if she had a number for her. When there was no answer at the house, I called the bar. They said Mama hadn't been in all night, and Eddie had just left. I finally reached Eddie at the house. He said Mama was gone. Said she'd taken some cash and left him."

"You don't believe him?"

The cynical twist of her lips revealed the woman she had become. "Would you?"

"I don't believe anybody."

"Me, neither."

"When was that?"

She counted back mentally, avoiding Nick's gaze. "Five, six, maybe eight weeks."

"That's a long time for happiness to last."

At least in the world they'd come from.

"When's the last time you talked to your sister?"

Guilt made her gaze flit about the room again. "She called me about three, four months ago. We didn't talk much." She shrugged, hating that she still felt the need to ask for absolution. "Same old, same old. She needed money. I sent it." She was almost afraid to ask. "You know anything about her? Maybe where I can find her?"

"She was hanging out at a place called Mother's down lower South Street."

"Near the port?"

"I'll find her," he said.

Stay out of it, she heard in his tone. She threw him her best low look of warning. He gave it right back to her.

"I used to walk these streets too, Fiore."

"Yeah, in K-mart closeouts." His gaze raked over her body and her five-hundred dollar French outfit.

He had a point. That pissed her off even more. "Hey, I wasn't the only one who got my butt kicked from one end of Lansing to the other on more than one occasion."

"Stay away from the port."

He'd tried to tell her what to do. He'd made a big mistake.

He took out a business card. ''Where are you staying?''

She had no idea. When she'd called and learned her mother was missing, she'd used her frequent flier miles to take the first available commuter, then a taxi to her mother and stepfather's house where she'd found only ''Cherry'' and her bald-headed, beer-bellied stepfather in his boxers. She hadn't thought any further ahead than that. She wasn't going to stay at her stepfather's. She didn't know who was left in the old neighborhood.

''I'll get a hotel room.''

''They just put up a new Americana downtown a few months ago. You have a cell phone?''

She nodded.

''Write it down. Your sister, your mother have that number?''

She slanted her gaze. ''Mama had my old number. My cell got stolen a few weeks ago. I meant to call and give her the new number…''

He glanced up. No sympathy, no reproach and she was grateful.

''Mama always called the apartment anyway.''

He wrote on the card. ''On the front is the station house number. This is my cell and my pager number on the back. Call in your room number when you get one. I'll bring Jo Jo to you.'' He stood. ''In the meantime, hang out at the hotel, order some room service and a chick flick and paint your toenails. Nothing worse on a woman than ugly toes.''

Damn if he hadn't done it again—ordered her

around. She was getting steamed even if the things this man did with toes were almost worth excusing his arrogance. "She's my mother, Nick."

"Whatever happened, it's not your fault, Cissy."

"I know that." But it sure felt like it.

"Have any recent pictures of your mother on you?"

"And you almost had me guilt-free here."

"We'll need one. I'll start looking for Jo Jo, stop by your stepfather's bar and talk to Eddie. C'mon." He touched her arm with a carefulness she didn't remember. "I'll walk you out."

"Besides being a righter of wrongs, got any other good surprises for me, Fiore?" she asked as they left the station house, crossed into the parking lot. "Married?"

"I'm not that much of a changed man." He spotted the Thunderbird. "You're driving your mother's car?"

"I'm borrowing it." They reached the car. She slid into the driver's seat.

He moved between the open door and the car. "What about you?"

"What about me what?"

"Married?"

"Once. Until he broke my jaw. So much for true love." She shrugged. "Like mother, like daughter, huh?"

He shook his head, telling her no. Mercifully the black of his eyes stayed hard, flat. She wouldn't accept otherwise from him.

"Well, I did take the Limoges vase we'd gotten from his Aunt Georgine as a wedding present and gave him a concussion."

"You always did have a classy way about you." He smiled, a compatriot, and she remembered why she'd let him get into her pants.

"A cop and a Wall Street wheeler-dealer."

She didn't correct him. "Who'd have thought it when we were young?"

For a second, the black eyes softened. "We were never young, Spagnola."

He looked at her so long her insides hummed like a hive. He was a crazy-maker.

"You ever have a cop before, Spagnola?"

Bless him. She shook her head, straining to hear him above the purr.

He closed her door. "Yeah, you did."

"That didn't count."

He ran the back of his finger down her cheek. "Yeah, it did." He grinned, shut the car door.

She fastened her seat belt.

LOWER DOWNTOWN had once been a wasteland of low-income housing, abandoned buildings, small inner-city businesses with bars across their windows. But a revitalization fueled by district representatives eager to get one step closer to the governor's mansion sitting high in the distance and an influx of single young professionals had made the area fashionably urban in the past few years.

Now town houses alternated with crack houses.

Hookers complained to city hall about the lack of decent parking. Still, the renewal had not reached to where Cissy was headed. The warehouses were flat brown or a sad yellow and had the look of abandonment whether they were or not. The barges sat heavy and still in the gray-green water and the smell of fish and fruit and longshoremen's sweat wafted through the car's vents. Despite the heat and lack of air-conditioning, she'd left the top up and only the back windows cracked. She hadn't spent two hundred clams on a haircut to let nature have its way. Still the sweat trickling down her sides was from more than the summer heat. No one knew except her and an overpriced therapist, even fewer would believe it, but she hated to drive.

She parked in a lot several streets over from the docks, locked the car and started toward a squat, flat-roofed building with a neon Miller sign in one window and Mother's in faded blue letters above its door. She had changed her clothes from well-heeled Wall Street to denim and one-hundred percent cotton, charged at B. Lodge's uptown. She figured that concession was close enough to obeying Nick's orders to stay away from the port.

She stepped into the bar, stopping to adjust to the darkness after the day's bright sun. For that second, she wished she didn't always feel compelled to do the opposite of whatever she was told to do. Even in common denim and white cotton and Keds, she was as conspicuous as a hungry starlet.

She made a beeline for the bar, inviting the men to

go back to their dart games and their beer and their alcohol-induced sense that nothing was amiss.

The bartender was beefy and bald with a beard that hung halfway down his chest in obvious overcompensation to the lack of hair on his head. He had the massive biceps of a weightlifter, and Cissy suspected that on two-dollar draft night, he doubled as a bouncer. She counted five tattoos on his left arm alone before he growled, "What can I do you for?"

He threw a cardboard coaster on the cracked Naugahyde counter. She appreciated the attempt at ambiance. She slung herself onto a stool as if she were a regular and smiled to show him there was no reason why they couldn't be friends.

He folded his arms, crushing his beard to his chest. The rattlesnake inked down his right arm seemed to unfurl.

"I was told I might be able to find Jo Jo Spagnola here."

"That right? Who told you that?"

She hesitated and was instantly outed. The man's eyes narrowed. Nick was right. She'd kept sharp dealing with the daily roller-coaster ride of Wall Street, the early-learned practice of trusting no one and showing no fear making her seem born to broker. But she'd been away from these streets too long.

She had just matched the man's mean squint when something flickered in his red-rimmed gaze.

"Cissy?"

She kept her own stare hard. "Maybe."

The man's meaty lips smiled. "Cissy Spagnola."

Cissy concentrated on the man's face, but nothing clicked.

"It's me, Billy. Billy Silverman."

"Billy Silverman?" She remembered a sunken-chested bean of a boy whose butt was kicked up and down Lansing ten times more than Nick and hers put together.

The fleshy smile widened. "Actually they call me 'Big Bill' now."

"Makes sense," she agreed.

"A little Marines. A little steroids, and ba-da-bing."

"Ba-da-bing." Cissy echoed.

He wiped several sticky rings off the bar. "What can I get ya? It's on the house."

It wasn't much past noon and the strongest drink she'd had in the past ten years was a nonfat latte. "Double snakebite." She wasn't about to lose any freshly gained ground.

"So, what brings you home?" Big Bill set the shot in front of her.

She supposed if she'd ever really had a home, this city would come the closest. "What else?" She picked up the glass, her eyes crossing from the drink's fumes. "Family."

"What always," he agreed with a truly pained expression for a man with a dagger dripping blood down his forearm.

"Hear, hear," she toasted. Big Bill watched her closely. It was now or never. She'd been gone too long and too far to be trusted on the basis of old times alone. *This one's for you, Ma.* She swallowed the drink in one gulp. She smacked her lips, released a satisfied "A-h-h." She still had it.

"Looking for little sis, huh?" Bill picked up her glass for a refill. Her pleasure at her performance waned.

"The last number I have for her is no longer in service. I heard she hung here."

"She in trouble?"

She told him the truth. "I don't know."

"She never seems to stray far from it." He set another shot in front of her and leaned against the back counter.

Cissy recognized the challenge. In this neighborhood, proving yourself was part of the game. She eyed the drink. Two of these on an empty stomach and Gentleman George, who she'd seen still set up camp on the city's corners with an almost elegant woven basket for change and a paper bag of Mad Dog 20-20, would be suave compared to her. Still, she needed info and she hadn't gotten any. On the other hand, Big Bill could be calling her bluff. They'd both played the game. She reached for the drink. On principle alone, she never backed away from a dare.

She had the glass to her lips when Big Bill circled her wrist with his callused palm. "'Scrappy Cissy.' You never could resist playing with the big boys, could you?"

She looked up from the upside-down cross, signature tattoo of the motorcycle gang, the Lords, inked on Bill's inner forearm. "Story of my life, Big Bill."

He downed the drink himself. "I heard you did pretty good. Jo Jo, she was always going on about you."

Compared to her younger sister's mixed-up life, Gentleman George was a success story.

Big Bill poured himself another shot. "Jo Jo was real proud of you."

The guilt was as familiar as it was keen. She'd stayed away with acceptable excuses but she knew the real reason she rarely came home. She was afraid—afraid of the helplessness she experienced every time she thought of her sister, her mother. Afraid of the small chant that came every time she saw them. *There but for the grace of God...* Now her mother was missing, her sister obviously still strung out, and she, the prodigal daughter, right back where she began—broke, frustrated, burning for more than her barely blue-collar roots. And, as illustrated by her earlier reaction to a man who had ruined more women than a cheap bikini wax, not one iota wiser.

"Listen, I'll tell you what I told Fiore—"

"Nick's been here already?" Not that it mattered, she reminded herself. Besides a moment of insanity when she'd married her slimeball first husband, she'd never let anyone tell her what to do.

"You kept up with Nick?" He eyed her slyly. "You two used to cha-cha, no?"

"It was once—"

Big Bill lifted bushy eyebrows.

"Hey—" She'd given up the virgin act readily long ago when she learned what awaited on the other side. Still, nine years of Sunday school and no patent leather shoes during her formative years was hard to break. "What do you know about it anyway?"

Big Bill shrugged. "Nothing. Fiore 'cha-cha'-ed every skirt I knew. Just checking to see if it'd been a clean sweep."

"Where's my sister, Billy?"

Her tone was too close to "cut the crap." Big Bill's gaze went into caution mode. She knew what he was thinking. *Scrappy Cissy.*

Sunken-chested butt-kicked bean boy, she mentally threw right back.

Big Bill heaved a sigh. The skull earring in his right ear shimmied. "All right."

One for scrappy Cissy.

"I'll tell you what I told Nick. Nick. A cop. Can you beat that?"

"I'm still trying to wrap my mind around it. So where can I find Jo Jo?"

"She worked here for about two months…when she showed up. Most of the time if she did show, she was too lit up to be any use to me anyway, but she'd start singing the blues and well, her and I, we go back some."

Cissy nodded. Like most addicts, her sister was a master of manipulation. It was a survival skill. Even aware of it, Cissy herself had let her sister work her over more than once.

"She hung out off and on with a dude who worked the tankers. Name's Saint-Sault. He'd come up from New Orleans but he was Canadian. Smooth dog.

Threw a lot of money around whenever the ship docked in the port.''

''He still around?''

''He comes and goes. Haven't seen him in a while. Haven't seen Jo Jo either. Couple weeks ago, I caught her taking cash out of the register and pocketing it. Had to let her go. She got all huffy, as if I had some nerve firing her because she was stealing me blind. She's a real piece of work, that one.''

''She's a classic. And you haven't seen her since?''

''A few nights ago, stopped by your father's joint—''

''He's *not* my father.''

The big man raised his hands, her point made. ''Wednesday, I think it was.''

''You talk to her?''

Big Bill shook his head. ''No, I stayed away. Your mother was serving that night. She and your little sister, they seemed to be having a 'discussion.' Then Jo Jo stomped out, not looking too happy. Nor too healthy.''

''My mom was working a Wednesday? Last time I talked to her, she was only working Friday and Saturday nights.''

Big Bill shrugged. ''Maybe she was filling in for one of the other girls. Picking up a little spare cash.''

For the new house? Or a new life?

''What was Saint-Sault's first name?''

''Jacques. He busted a guy's nose one night for calling him 'Jock.'''

"Sounds like a sweetheart. He and Jo Jo like to hang out anywhere else?"

"Anywhere there was action, if they're still hanging together. One of the regulars last week said they'd seen Jo Jo at a place uptown. The Golden Cue. But she wasn't with Saint-Sault."

Cissy slid off the stool, pulling out the twenty she'd found stuffed between the car's front seat cushions when she'd searched for the seat belt. "Thanks, Big Bill."

"Hey, I told you it's on the house."

Cissy hesitated. She didn't like accepting favors. Time come they'd be called in. But a perceived insult could be just as deadly. She worked to appear gracious.

"Okay, well, thanks again."

"How long you in town?"

"I'm not sure." She looked into Big Bill's eyes, the size and shade of rabbit pellets. "A while, I guess." She scribbled her cell number on a cocktail napkin. "If you see Jo Jo, will you give her this? Tell her I'm looking for her."

Big Bill enjoyed watching her walk to her car. He watched as she got into her car, jumped right back out, her mouth working while she took down the car's convertible top. Still talking to herself, she got back in, checked the side and rear mirrors, then drove out of sight. He waited another minute before he picked up the phone.

Chapter Two

Nick checked out the Golden Cue, noting windows, exits, alarms. The décor was uptown, but its roots were from down the line. Like Cissy.

He scanned the people inside the pool hall, studied the man wearing arm garters behind the bar. All looked routine, but that meant nothing to Nick. He trusted nothing or no one, a trait that made for a solitary man but a great cop. He moved toward the bar.

"What can I get you, sir?" The bartender slid an eight-ball coaster across the bar. He was medium height, 180 pounds, blond hair, blue eyes and an angle to his nose that suggested it'd been broken more than once.

Nick flashed his shield. "I'm looking for someone."

The bartender looked at the badge, unimpressed.

"Jo Jo Spagnola."

"What about her?"

"Know her?"

"She comes in here sometimes, shoots the breeze until her boyfriend arrives."

"Got a name for the boyfriend?"

The bartender shook his head. "He stayed in the back at the tables."

"Jo Jo never mentioned his name?"

"Someone wants to tell me something, I listen. They don't, I don't ask."

"What'd he look like?"

The other man shrugged. "Not much. Thirty something. Suit-and-tie guy. Pale looking, like he didn't get outside much. Kind of nondescript, you know. One of those guys that blends. Except for the hair. Guy had good hair."

"Good hair?"

"Thick. Shone like mink under the table lights. Obvious dye job, but a good one. Must have had it done professionally. I figured the low profile for the fact he was married."

"That's what you think was going on with this guy and Jo Jo? An affair?"

"Maybe. I don't know. Guy didn't seem her type, but then, what do I know?"

"Jo Jo ever meet anyone else here?"

The bartender shook his head.

"How 'bout her boyfriend?"

"Yeah, he met somebody else."

"Another woman?"

"Businessman."

"Let me guess. No name."

"You got it. Always came in late, after midnight, sat in the back. Sherry, waitress who worked the night shift, never left early when they walked in. They were good tippers.''

"Sherry still working here?"

The bartender shook his head. "Left last month. Moved with a cousin to California.''

"This other businessman, what'd he look like?"

"Dark. Thick waisted. Expensive suit. Respectable looking.''

"And they came in late, sat in the back and that was it.''

"Yeah, pretty quiet for a boys' night out, except last time they were in.''

"What happened?''

"The jukebox was playing, but I could hear their voices coming from the back. They were arguing about something.''

"You hear what?''

"Not over the music. Neither looked too happy when they left, though. Haven't seen the other man in here again.''

"What about Jo Jo and her boyfriend?''

"They were in last week.''

"What day?''

"Tuesday, Wednesday, maybe Thursday.''

"That's the last time you've seen either of them?''

The bartender nodded. "Something happen to Jo Jo?''

"That's what we're trying to find out. Thanks for your time." Nick laid a card on the bar. "You think of something else or see Jo Jo or her friend, this is my number.''

Nick walked to the unmarked sedan parked on the street, unlocked the front door. With the air conditioner going full blast, he pulled out into traffic and headed back downtown. Big Bill had been right. Jo Jo had been at the Golden Cue with someone else. According to Big Bill, Saint-Sault was tall, had a blond ponytail and hadn't been seen in a while. Perhaps someone at the port had seen him. He neared Mother's again on his way to the docks, saw a bright red Thunderbird, top down, pulling out in the opposite direction. The fact that the woman in the car looked beautiful with her long hair blowing only pissed Nick off more as he pulled a U-turn.

CISSY WAS SITTING at a red light when her purse on the passenger seat rang. She fumbled inside it, pulled out her cell phone.

"Cissy Spagnola."

"Go home."

"I am home." Her response surprised her as much as the threatening voice on the other end. "Who is this?"

The line went dead. She listened to the silence while her mind worked, trying to place the voice that thought it could push her around. It had been muffled, purposely disguised. She tossed the cell on top of her purse. The light turned green. As she pressed on the gas, her phone rang again. She grabbed it greedily.

"Listen, peckerhead—" Whoever it was wasn't getting a second chance to scare the pants off her.

"Talking on a handheld cell phone while driving in this state is illegal."

Nick. Who had used different tactics to get her pants off her.

She glanced in the rearview mirror for a department vehicle, but saw nothing. "How do you know I'm even driving?"

"Hang up and pull over."

She still hadn't adjusted to Nick's voice, real, growling and calling up images she preferred to shred. "Are you tailing me?" That hum had to be in her cell phone. A pelvis couldn't purr like that.

"Don't even attempt lingo." She heard his disgust.

"I don't see a police car."

"The light you're heading for just turned red."

She shifted her gaze, slammed on the brake. "I still don't see a police car," she argued, peering again in the mirror. "It wouldn't be the first time you lied to me."

A Harley-Davidson motorcycle pulled up on her driver's side. The rider wore a button-down shirt and tie, tailored pants and a black helmet. He turned his head, his face covered by full visor. He twisted the accelerator handle. The engine roared. Cissy couldn't see the driver's face but she knew beneath that opaque Plexiglas, he was smiling. Manopause.

The sun flashed off the bike's chrome, polished to perfection with muscle and love. A metallic gleam moved, lifted, aimed. Cissy stared almost in fascination. A tidy little gun pointed at her forehead. Her brows pulled together, asking that gunbarrel's black hole, "What the—?" She twisted the wheel and drove onto the sidewalk, beeping her horn as pedestrians scattered and swore at her in curses she'd learned in childhood. From her phone thrown on the seat, she heard Nick screaming a similar litany.

"Oh yeah," she yelled above her horn and wheels squealing. "At least now you can't arrest me for talking on my cell phone, can you?" She veered into Maiden at the corner, the street angling toward the preserve. Her lane was blocked by a double-parked Acura. A garbage truck took up the opposite lane. Cissy glanced wildly at the sidewalk. A woman was pushing a baby carriage, the heat and the hill making her face shine.

Cissy leaned on the horn. The uniformed man slinging the trashcans into the truck's jaws gave her the finger. She looked in the rearview mirror, saw the cycle, its faceless driver. The motorcycle pulled up flush at the driver's door. The metallic length throwing rainbows in the high heat, aimed at her. She pressed on the gas, shot for the slender space between the Acura and the garbage truck, knew she'd never make it. She held the gas pedal to the floor. "C'mon, Cherry," she prayed. "Make Mama proud."

She watched the Acura's driver's door opening as if in slow motion, one stockinged leg in heels stretching out. "No," she screamed, leaning on the horn. She slammed on the brake, wished she could close her eyes. The trash men were standing around, watching as if on afternoon break. The leg, so lovely it only pissed Cissy off more, jerked back. She heard a thud as she was thrown against the seat. Metal screamed as the Acura's door was ripped off its hinges. It flew up into the air as if celebrating freedom only to fall, bounce on the asphalt like a pitched penny. God, she hated driving.

She glanced in the rearview mirror to see the motorcycle corner into a side alley. Three-L-Z was all she got on the plate. A dark unmarked sedan, its headlights flashing, rounded the opposite corner.

She grabbed her cell phone. "Hey, what happened to black and white? Blue and yellow? Big, bold letters, City Police?"

As if in answer, a black-and-white patrol car turned in from the other corner.

"Pull over, Cissy."

"With pleasure."

She pulled up to the curb behind a vintage VW Beetle, watched Nick get out of the car and come toward her. Over the years she'd wondered if she might have exaggerated his handsomeness, his raw energy. She hadn't. Now with a gun strapped to his side, the man knew no mercy.

The luckily saved leg in the Acura had been joined by another that went all the way up to an indecently short skirt, a shirt with shoestring straps and a mane of bottle-blond hair. Another patrol car pulled up at the opposite end to block off the street. Two uniformed men directed traffic. Another two followed Nick to the Acura. Hot Legs was pacing back and forth, gesturing at the empty space where the door had been. The garbage men who had raced to her side, gallant knights smelling of sweat and refuse, gathered round her, offering comfort. Nick stopped, must have said something reassuring or sexy, because Hot Legs went still a moment, tossed her obviously dyed tresses and smiled up at him, all teeth and mouth. The garbage men got their money's worth. The woman was still all teeth as Nick nodded to the two other policemen and headed toward the Thunderbird.

Cissy gazed straight ahead, her hands sweaty, gripping the steering wheel until the tap on the windshield.

She turned, coming face-to-face with Nick Fiore for the second time that day and knowing she'd never get used to the sensation.

"Driver's license and registration."

"You're playing with me, aren't you?"

His stoic silence told her nothing.

"Why are you hanging around harassing innocent citizens anyway?"

His eyebrows lifted on "innocent."

"That guy. That slimeball on the motorcycle. He had a gun and he was about to use me for target practice. Didn't you see that?"

"I was busy watching you tear up city property and terrorize pedestrians."

"He had a gun."

He studied her as if gauging her sanity.

"He was going to shoot me."

He looked down at her, the black in his eyes darker than she remembered. She didn't realize she was trembling until he touched her upper arm. She jerked away.

"I'm telling you, there's an insane businessman on a bike running around this city, and he's got a bullet with my name on it."

He turned and went back to his vehicle.

"Hey!" She jumped out of the car, slammed the door hard enough to make Cherry's bones rattle.

"We'll need your information, ma'am," the uniformed cop standing beside Hot Legs noted as Cissy marched by.

"And insurance policy number," the blonde added.

Cissy ignored them both and headed toward the sedan. It swerved to miss her and sped off in the direction the motorcycle had headed.

The patrol officer came up beside her. "License and registration, ma'am."

The sedan disappeared. Cissy stared after it as helpless as when a gun had been aimed at her head.

"BLACK HARLEY LAST SEEN heading northbound down Glen. Driver five-ten, 160 pounds, business clothing, black helmet with tinted full-face front visor. May be armed."

Too much time had passed. A motorcycle was easily slipped into a side alley or a parking garage. The gunman could be strolling the street already, blending with the lunch-hour crowd, or within minutes he could have exchanged the motorcycle for something four-wheeled and more respectable. Businessmen clandestinely meeting in billiard halls; a man in a suit chases down a car in broad daylight. The moves were getting bolder—an indication the bad guys were getting desperate. And when things got desperate, people died.

Nick slammed his fist against the steering wheel. Fists. Just like his old man. Sometimes it was all he knew. A red rage he had fought his whole life to control. In the choice of a profession that demanded restraint, cautious use of power. In the choice of a personal life that allowed no one to get too close.

He hadn't even seen a gun. He had been too focused on Cissy. The girl had rattled him, taken him off his game. He didn't like it.

One shot, and Cissy could have been lying in the street right now. Dead. His fist slammed the wheel.

CISSY WAS AT NICK'S SIDE before he could open the door.

"Did you get a license plate?" Nick asked her.

"You lost him?" He'd left her behind, and she didn't like it.

"A motorcycle is easy to get rid of, replace with something else. Patrols are on the lookout."

"I caught some of the plate. Three-L-Z."

"Partial plate three, *L* as in lion, *Z* as in zebra," Nick called in. "Again, suspect possibly armed."

"No 'possibly' about it," Cissy protested. "The scumbag is packing."

A thin vein popped out on Nick's temple. He got out of the car. He stood a head and a half taller than her and was probably double her weight. Okay, one and one-half times her weight. With a hard exhale communicating she was peeved, she straightened to her full five foot four inches.

"Why would a businessman on a black Harley want to kill you, Cissy?"

She put one hand on her hip, cocked it as she took a step toward him to let him know she wasn't going to be intimidated. Attracted, yeah. Purring like the little engine that could. But badge and big, beautiful body aside, Nick Fiore wasn't going to tell her what to do. She'd gotten careless once, let a man try to push her around. It wouldn't happen again. "You're the cop. You tell me."

"Maybe someone besides me didn't like the fact you went down to Mother's and started asking questions."

"My mother and sister are missing. I'm not going to sit around a motel room."

Nick sighed, rubbed one side of his head.

She smiled. "You still do that, huh?"

"What?"

"Rub the side of your head when you're frustrated."

"You've seen this move before?"

"I've seen all your moves, Fiore."

He broke out into the slow-coming grin that was move numero uno in Cissy's book.

"Somebody did call me after I left Mother's," she said before any more moves surfaced, and she could no longer think straight. "The one you called to harass me about. The voice was deliberately disguised."

"What'd it say?"

"'Go home.'"

"Not exactly a warm welcome back, is it?"

"I didn't expect a party."

They stood, shoulders set, stance ready to attack. To an outsider, from the firm mouths, the thrust of their chests, they could be enemies. But in their locked gazes, they were allies.

He nodded toward the blonde and the patrol officers. "They get everything they need?"

"I was on my way to look for the insurance cards when you pulled in."

They started toward the others.

"Look. Look at this car." Hot Legs had worked herself into a lather.

"I'm sorry," Cissy offered.

"I could've been killed."

"Me, too," Cissy said.

Hot Legs gave a huff.

"We'll need your license and proof of insurance, ma'am," the uniformed policeman told her.

"I hope you have good coverage," Hot Legs let her know.

"Isn't double parking illegal?" Cissy wondered aloud. She headed toward Cherry, praying the insurance cards were in the car somewhere.

The Thunderbird's headlight was shattered, the metal around it wrinkled, paint scraped off the side. She patted the car's hood like an old friend. "We're not having a good day, are we?"

She opened the passenger-side door and slid in,

throwing her purse onto the driver's seat. She clicked open the glove compartment, shuffled through packs of matches, odd pens, a compact, a map folded wrong, a coupon for a free cocktail on Ladies' Night at the Hideaway. A half-full bottle of nail polish rolled out as she dug deep. Beneath a Garth Brooks CD, she found a plastic orange sleeve, the insurance company's business card tucked in its front and the insurance cards inside. She resisted the urge to lay a big wet one on the slick orange cover. She shoved the cards into her purse, crammed everything else back into the glove box and closed it. She grabbed her purse and was sliding out when she saw the dark color oozing onto the floor. The nail polish's cap must have been loosened from the fall. Polish was leaking onto the carpet.

"Oh, hell." She slammed her purse on the seat, grabbed several napkins out of the glove compartment and threw them on the wet spot. She grabbed another handful of napkins, slid out, got on her knees and leaned in to sop up the spill.

"Problem?" Nick asked behind her.

"A bottle of nail polish leaked all over the floor. I've got most of the color wiped up, although at this point, it doesn't seem—" She stopped as, stuffed beneath the passenger seat, she saw two neatly banded stacks of cash.

She jerked upright, banging her head on the open glove compartment. A hand reached over her shoulder. She gave a start.

"I'll take care of those," Nick said.

She looked down at the napkins wadded in her fist, plopped them into Nick's palm while trying to understand the fact that a couple of substantial bundles of cash were crammed beneath the seat beside her.

"You okay?"

"Sure, sure." She pushed herself up, brushed off her shorts. Nick studied her. *Trained to suspect.*

"That stuff, whoa, the smell made me a little dizzy." She fumbled in her purse, avoiding Nick's study. "I found the insurance cards. Ta-dum." She brandished them out of her bag.

He pitched the napkins into a trash can on the sidewalk, reached for the insurance cards. He motioned for the other cop to come over. "I need your driver's license, too."

She whipped out her wallet, slid out her license and handed it to him.

He studied the card, shook his head.

"Yes, I know. The perm was a mistake."

He looked at her. "This license expired seven months ago."

"No way." She grabbed the card out of his hand, read the date. "Well, obviously somebody forgot to send me a renewal. Not that it matters much. I never drive. Owning a car in the city is only a grand theft waiting to happen."

"You were driving today." He sighed. "Come on."

"Come on where?"

"It's illegal to drive without a license."

"I'll go right to the DMV and straighten this all out. And I'll take the bus."

"You were driving illegally and hit a parked car."

"Double-parked," she corrected.

His gaze stayed steady on her. "People willingly give you their hard-earned money?"

Not anymore. But only she and the washed-up firm of Banes Brokerage knew that. She resisted the urge to retort "The city legally gave you a gun?" Whether it was Nick Fiore or not, antagonizing a member of the local law enforcement would not be the smoothest move she'd made in the past week.

"Let's go, Spagnola."

"What about the car?" And the twin stacks of cash beneath the front seat?

"It'll be towed."

"What? You think I'm stupid?"

He tipped a corner of his mouth. Move twenty-three, if Cissy remembered right.

"I know the routine. Those guys court the cops, then charge triple to the poor saps who get towed."

"Someone might have tried to take you out during their lunch break and you're worried about a trumped-up towing charge?"

No, she was worried about her mother, her sister, threatening phone calls, a motorcycle-riding mystery man with a gun, and now wads of cash stuffed under the front seat. But until she knew more, she preferred to keep this latest discovery to herself.

Nick massaged the back of his neck. "Give me the keys. I'll have one of the officers drive it over to my garage and tell the owner I'll be over later to talk to him. In the meantime, I'll drop you off at the DMV. Considering the circumstances, I'll overlook the fines for the expired license, but I'm not letting you behind the wheel again until I have proof you're legal.''

Nick's solution was too reasonable to protest. Still, as he started toward the others, she stayed rooted while her mind worked overtime to find an excuse. He glanced over his shoulder, saw she wasn't following.

He took a long breath. ''I do have handcuffs.''

''Are you trying to ask me out on a date?''

His eyes warned her she was walking a fine line.

''You were more fun before you became a cop.''

Now he smiled. ''You were more fun before I became a cop, too.''

He'd won. And he knew it.

''Just let me check that spill, see if I can blot up a little more Flamboyant Fuchsia.'' She grabbed napkins out of the glove compartment and knelt down, setting her handbag on the floor beside the dried stain. She patted the floor a few times, then, making sure her body blocked Nick's view, she darted her hand under the seat, scooped one stack, then the other into her purse. Thank God she had always opted for small suitcases instead of the envelope-sized clutches so chic nowadays. She snapped her purse shut and stood.

''Ready?'' Nick asked behind her.

She had the cash. Now all she had to do was find her mother and her sister and stay one step ahead of scumbags with a fondness for motorcycles and shiny guns. Was that what her mother and sister were doing? Staying one step ahead of someone who wanted them dead? Had they succeeded? Her legs felt suddenly unsteady. She needed something to lean on.

"Don't make me use force, Spagnola."

She turned to Nick's hard expression. The shakiness subsided. She blessed him for the second time that day.

"Easy, Officer. I'll come willingly." She moved toward him. "Just like ol' times."

He smiled as he escorted her to the sedan, its lights still flashing like a Mardi Gras. "You said it yourself, Cissy." He opened the car's back door and stood waiting for her to enter as if this were the prom night they'd never had.

"People don't change."

Chapter Three

As soon as the car door slammed, she began to shake. She clutched her handbag on her lap, the bulk adding no comfort. She pressed her molars to each other, locked her jaw and focused on the clean edge of Nick's hairline in front of her.

"Why would a man on a motorcycle want to kill me?" She leaned toward that precise line bisecting Nick's nape.

"I asked you first."

She clasped her purse. The trembling traveled up and down the biceps she'd always thought of as scrawny. "And that phone call." She flexed her arms to still the shaking and give her some sense of dignity. The pathetic results were the opposite.

"Someone wants you out of Dodge."

She slumped back against the seat. "Why would anyone want to kill me?" she repeated with such fresh incredulity she expected a smart remark from Nick.

"Maybe he wasn't trying to kill you."

"The man had a gun, Nick."

"Maybe he was trying to scare you. Give you a warning."

"Like the phone call?" Cissy considered.

"Maybe whatever is going on, you're in the way. An unnecessary complication."

Cissy studied her old lover's neck, the back of his head strong but with an elegance of form and shape he probably despised. A shaved nape, and she was sweating. She looked away, fed up with herself. It wasn't as if she hadn't had her share of men. Granted, none as memorable as Nick—except for her ex-husband, who remained infamous in her memory for completely different reasons. She stared out the window, watched the buildings of her past go by.

"Or maybe our Harley-riding fast-tracker thought you were someone else."

"Like who?"

"The car's owner."

"My mother?"

"Maybe your mother saw something, knows something she's not supposed to. Maybe the bad guys know she drives a red 1950 Thunderbird."

"If the bad guy thought it was Mama driving Cherry, then that would mean my mother *is* still out there, somewhere, alive."

"It's a theory," Nick cautioned. "That's all. Some thinking out loud until we catch a break." He glanced in the mirror at her. "You named the car?"

"My mother did." She leaned forward. "Did you go talk to Eddie?"

"I went to the bar, but he hadn't shown up yet.

One of the guys taking a brewery delivery said he usually didn't show up during the week until later. I made a few other stops, was on my way to the docks when I saw 'Cherry' pulling out by Mother's.'' In the rearview mirror, she saw his lip curl. ''Surprise, surprise.''

''What'd you learn on your 'other' stops?''

''That's confidential information on an ongoing investigation.''

''I'll bet it gives you a buzz to say that.'' She sank into the seat. ''Do you think they're alive, Nick? My mother and sister?'' She met his gaze in the mirror, the black eyes that rarely revealed. She had expected anything but silence. It scared her most of all.

''I can't answer that, Cissy.''

She looked away to the street, from one past to another.

''Not yet.''

She heard his promise. She found his eyes again in the mirror and was glad she had loved him once.

''Here we are.'' The car pulled up in front of a wide one-story building with a large parking lot. Nick turned to her. ''Go get legal again. I've got to go back to the station, fill out reports, check on some things. I'll pick you up in about an hour. When you get done, don't go anywhere. Stay right here until I get back.''

He'd done it again. Told her what to do. Halfway out the door, she whipped around, ready to do battle and caught the concern in those eyes that never told anything. Quick as she'd caught him, the eyes went blank. Her defiance fell. It'd been a long time since concern had come her way. Nick Fiore was the least likely source. *Surprise, surprise.*

''Behave yourself,'' he told her. ''You go getting yourself offed, and I'll have to go back down to the precinct and fill out a mess of paperwork.''

She smiled as she slid out of the car. ''I just might fall in love with you yet.''

The DMV had gone twenty-first century with a neon board that stated in red lights which number was being served. Tubular lights, pointing heavenward, blinked on with a soft chime beside the clerk that would process the next request. The woman at the front desk had explained that since Cissy's expiration was less than two years old, she could renew using the regular procedure. She filled out the necessary paperwork and sat down on one of the benches in long rows in the center of the room. Cissy focused on a clerk with a face as thin as his tie, but she thought about the man on the motorcycle, saw again the slender, almost elegant silver length of the gun rising, aiming. A chime sounded. Cissy jumped. Her number was flashing on the neon board. She got up, moved toward the counter.

The clerk, a middle-aged woman with thinning hair and a blank expression, slid Cissy's paperwork across the counter without looking up at her, reviewed it, checking the various boxes and blanks to make sure they had been filled in correctly. ''Please look at the eye chart on the wall and read the lowest line possible.''

Cissy read the letters on the chart. ''Step to the left,

place your feet on the footsteps,'' the clerk instructed without looking at her.

Cissy did as told, involuntarily patting her hair. She showed her teeth. ''I don't have anything in my teeth, do I?''

The camera blinked in answer.

''Hey, I wasn't ready. Redo.''

The woman gave her a flat gaze before she moved back to her station. ''This isn't Olan Mills.''

''Well, at least, it'll beat the 'do' on my last one. I looked like—''

''That'll be forty-three dollars.'' The clerk punctuated her request with the thud of a stamp. ''If you're writing a check, make it payable to—''

''I'm not writing a check,'' Cissy informed her. Her checking account balance had been decidedly unreliable since tech stocks went in the toilet.

She reached into her briefcase-size purse, fumbling for her wallet. Her fingers closed around the cash from Cherry's front seat. Cold cash was an inept expression. Even this mystery money was warm as a good memory.

''Credit card?'' the woman said, her gaze on the wall clock behind Cissy.

''Yes.'' Cissy snatched her hand away from the rubber-banded root of all evil and found her wallet. She pulled it out and opened it. A ten and four ones were in the cash compartment. Plastic cards lined the opposite side. She slipped one out and handed it to the clerk.

The woman walked to a counter behind her, slid

the card through for authorization. She walked back a minute later. "Declined." A note of superiority ingrained itself in the announcement.

Cissy grabbed the card. "Those Macy's one-day sales are going to kill me yet. Here." She swept another card out of her wallet. The clerk gazed down at it dubiously before taking it and walking to the back. Cissy crossed her fingers not to be done in by the DMV. The clerk came back with a credit slip for her to sign, and she breathed easy.

The clerk handed her a paper. "This is a temporary license. Your new license arrives in the mail in four to six weeks." The clerk pressed a button and the light above her desk gave a ping. Cissy jumped again. She stepped away from the counter, was slipping the temporary license in her wallet when she heard someone call her name.

She looked up, past the clerk.

"It's me." A buxom woman in rebellious orange amid the beige and the bland stepped out of one of the offices that banked the back of the service area. "Juanita Willis. Well, actually it's Juanita Carlucci now."

Juanita Willis. She'd taught Cissy how to French inhale and shorten the skirt of her school uniform by rolling up the waistband, but it was Cissy who had introduced her to Tommy Carlucci.

"Juanita!" Pleasure filled Cissy's voice as she smiled at her old friend. "You didn't actually go and marry that wild man, did you?"

"You know I did. And I've got the certificate from

the Viva Las Vegas Wedding Chapel, two kids, a raised ranch in the country and a fat black Lab to prove it.'' Juanita came through the counter's half door to hug Cissy. ''Give me a hug, girl, and lie to me and tell me I look good.''

Laughing, Cissy hugged her girlhood friend. ''Honey, believe me when I tell you you're a sight for sore eyes.''

''Let me look at you.'' Juanita leaned back to take Cissy in. She nodded her approval, linked her arm through Cissy's. ''Got a minute to catch up? I've got a half-eaten bag of red licorice twists and enough pictures of the kids in my wallet to make you beg for mercy.''

Cissy glanced out the windows to the parking lot. No sign of Nick.

Juanita noted Cissy's glance. ''Unless you have to get somewhere.''

''No, no,'' Cissy assured her. ''Nick's supposed to pick me up and I was just checking to see if he was waiting for me.''

''Nick Fiore?'' Juanita raised her brows and smiled slyly.

''It's not what you think.''

''I'm not thinking anything, because I know you're going to tell your old buddy Juanita everything.''

''Not until I see your kids.''

The two women went into Juanita's office and closed the door. Over licorice and with photos spread out on the desktop, Cissy filled Juanita in on the past twenty-four hours.

Juanita shook her head when Cissy finished, her face grave. "Tommy and I moved out of the city when the kids were born. We commute in for work, but we got a little place down in Edgemont. We've lost touch with what's going on in the old neighborhood. I wish there was some way I could help you."

Cissy looked at her old friend. "Actually, there might be." Cissy smiled. Juanita smiled back. They could have been eleven again, about to cut P.E. to sneak smokes down by the felt factory. A short time later, Cissy had the information she needed and the two friends hugged goodbye. Both were wise enough not to promise to stay in touch.

She went outside. The heat hit her head-on. She leaned against the gray building in the shade of the roof's overhang and waited for Nick. Thanks to Juanita, technology and a partial plate number, Cissy had learned the Harley was registered to Phillip Lester on Pleasant Pond Drive in a suburb west of the city. Nick hadn't fooled her with his paperwork excuse. He'd gone back to the station to run the partial plate and get a name and an address. He'd probably already paid a visit to Phillip Lester. Not that he'd let her know if he had learned anything. He'd made it clear she was supposed to sit back and let the police handle the case.

Fat chance.

Her T-shirt stuck to her back. Her purse hung heavy on her shoulder. She cast a subversive glance inside it. The cash lay there, unreal. The top bill showing was a twenty. She reached in, lifted its corner. Another twenty, and another, and another. Nice safe denomination. Common, unobtrusive, easy to change. She reached past the bundle to the next. Same bills, as far as she could tell, tied up neat as a Christmas present.

Had her mother been planning on leaving her father, and this was her means? If so, why would she leave it behind along with the car? Had she meant to get away but got no farther than her husband's wrath? Despite the heat, Cissy went cold all over. She spied Nick pulling into the parking lot. She slid her hand out of her purse, stepped out from beneath the overhang.

He stopped in front of her. Knowing there were no civilians or fellow officers to worry about, she opened the front door this time and climbed in.

"Are you legal?" he asked.

She turned her head, stretched her neck toward the cool air blasting from the air-conditioning vents. "Fine fat wad that'll do me. Or my mother or sister." She decided to tell him later about running into Juanita. "Have you heard anything? Did anyone spot the man on the motorcycle?"

Nick pressed the gas pedal. "We're investigating."

"Another fine fat wad." Cissy slumped against the seat. "What about Cherry?"

He threw her a glance. "Why do women have to name their cars?"

"Why do men have to grab their crotches?"

He smiled, looking for the first time as if he was enjoying himself. "One of the patrol officers drove

'Cherry,'—'' he said the name with resignation ''—to Al's Auto Palace.''

''Sounds swanky.''

''He'll fix her right and charge you a fair price. Al's a friend of mine.''

She turned toward him. ''You got a lot of friends, Fiore?''

''As many as I have enemies.''

''Occupational hazard?''

''I'm going to stop, get a couple of slices before we go see Al. Want anything?''

Typical man, Cissy thought. Change the subject if the talk turned to anything personal or that smacked of feelings. Nick had chosen food. Food, sex or football. The big three, varying in priority depending on the month and the time of day.

''Rocky's went out of business two years ago. The old man had a stroke and the one son sold the business. But Napoli's still has a decent pie.'' Nick swung onto Douglas.

Cissy would have preferred to go straight to the garage. She had only seen under the front seat on the passenger side, stuck her hand between the cushions on the driver's side when searching for the seat belt. Lord knew what other secrets Cherry might have. At least Cissy knew the trunk only held her overnight bag.

Her purse weighed heavy on her lap. She could tell Nick about the money. She gave him a sidelong glance, made herself get past his looks that made women lose their self-respect. Even before he'd been professionally trained, he'd learned not to trust. So had she. Until she knew more about what was going on and could take a better look inside the Thunderbird, she wasn't ready to confide in anyone. She rested both hands on her handbag.

Nick pulled over, parked about a half block from a dark red and green building with Pizza etched on the windows in neon.

They were almost to the building when someone called out Nick's name. They both turned to see a brown-haired man coming toward them. Despite the heat, the man wore a full suit. He had put on weight since Cissy had last had the pleasure, but she easily recognized Tommy Marcus. He had the kind of face that would have made him a good priest. It had been rumored once that his mother, Connie, God rest her soul, had had her fingers crossed. But instead, Tommy had gone off in search of a fortune and came back as close to heaven as one could get without the Pope's blessing—a rich man. Her mother had never failed to mention it. Her efforts had tripled after Cissy's divorce.

"Detective Fiore." The man held out his hand, included Cissy in his smile. He took a double take, his grin widening.

Cissy held out her hand. "How are you, Tommy?"

"Cissy? Cissy Spagnola?"

"In the flesh."

He pulled her into an embrace. "It's good to see you."

"Thanks. It's good to see you, too, Tommy. You're doing well, I hear. Congratulations."

He waved aside her compliments. "Everybody's got to make a living, right? So, how long you in town for? Or are you back for good?"

"I'm not sure," she answered honestly.

"Well, it's great to see you again. Hey, what about this guy?" He clamped his hand on Nick's shoulder. "How's the war going, Detective?"

"Depends on who's winning."

"I hope the good man, Detective. The good man."

"We're heading into Napoli's for some slices. Why don't you join us?" Nick invited.

"Sure, tempt me with Napoli's pie." Tommy patted his generous stomach. "Is that how he got you to come along?"

"No, he threatened to arrest me," Cissy replied.

"That's still a possibility," Nick warned.

"I knew there was a reason beautiful women hung out with you."

"Believe what you want, Marcus, but you need more than a big gun."

Marcus smiled. "Man's an animal. Much as I hate to pass on Napoli's, I have to speak at the Sons of Italy tonight, and if I show up full before the ladies have a chance to feed me, well—"

He didn't have to explain. Nick and Cissy understood an Italian woman's wrath when food was refused.

"Another time then."

"Most definitely." Tommy smiled at Cissy. "We've got to get together while you're in town."

"How's funding going for the Keeping It On the Courts program?" Nick asked.

"I've almost got Canestra to double it in this year's budget."

"Good work. Tell him he'll have the precinct's full support."

The two men shook hands. "Cissy," Tommy took her hand. "I really do hope we'll have time to catch up."

"I hope so, too," Cissy replied.

Tommy left. "Sounds like Tommy will be running for office himself someday," Cissy noted as she and Nick headed toward their restaurant.

"No one would be surprised if he did. He already hangs out with some political heavyweights, serves on the governor's advisory business board and has been involved in several neighborhood revitalization projects."

"What's 'Keeping It On the Courts?'"

"Inner city basketball program some of the guys at the station and myself coach. I got my cousin's son playing. My cousin was in his twenties when he was killed in a bar firebombing. He was out celebrating the birth of his firstborn. A boy."

"I'm sorry." She put her hand on his arm, felt the muscle tense beneath her touch.

"The boy's sixteen now and six foot five. We're working on a scholarship." He didn't shrug off her touch.

They went into the restaurant. Mama Napoli made a big fuss over both of them, called Guido out of the kitchen to see 'skinny little Cissy' all grown up, and refused to take their money.

They ate in the car, Nick maneuvering with one hand as he held a slice in the other.

Cissy took a final bite of crust. "So you didn't speak to Eddie yet?"

"I'm heading to the bar right after I take you over to Al's. I'll drop you off at your hotel on the way. Where are you staying?"

"I haven't decided."

He braked for a stop sign. "Well, decide and I'll drop you off after Al's."

The man would never learn.

When her silence grew long, he glanced at her. "I work alone, Cissy."

"You can either take me with you or drop me off at the next corner, and I'll get a taxi. Either way, I'm going to the tavern and see if I can find out what happened to my mother and my sister."

Nick eyed her. "I should have locked you up when I had the chance."

"Life is full of missed opportunities, Nick."

She ignored his glare. Men like Nick Fiore were dangerous but could be dealt with. All a girl had to remember was not to give an inch or she'd be a goner for sure.

"So, no news about that maniac on the motorcycle? And why he wanted to kill me?" she asked as if making conversation.

"Allegedly wanted to kill you."

She gave him a long look. "Tell that to the coroner."

"If you'd stay put in some hotel room, Harley-riding gunmen wouldn't have the chance to take a shot at you."

She crossed her arms, plopped them on her purse, the bundles of cash reminding her something very wrong and very dangerous was going on. And she intended to find out what.

"Do me a favor. Don't come to my funeral."

"Can I send flowers?"

If she hadn't been so mature, she would have called him a bad name. "No."

"A donation to your favorite charity?" He threw her a glance. "I'll make it a big one."

She threw in the bad name after all. Maturity wasn't all it was cracked up to be anyway.

Chapter Four

They pulled into the garage. Cissy went to the car to get her overnight bag while Nick walked into the bays. She waited until Nick was out of sight before looking under the seats, then, sliding her hand down the seat cushions as far as possible, searched for cash. She found a couple more bills in the driver's seat cushions and some change but no more fat stacks. Maybe her mother had been planning to leave her stepfather, and she'd kept a secret stash of money in her car like other women used a cookie jar. The only thing wrong with the whole theory was the car and the money were here and Louisa wasn't.

Cissy rechecked the trunk in case she'd overlooked anything before. Nothing but an umbrella and flashlight. She closed the trunk as Nick and a wiry, bald man in a greasy coverall came out of the garage. Nick introduced her and Cherry to Al. Al walked to Cherry's hood, ran a finger along the crumpled front end.

"I can work up an estimate, give you a call with the figure before I start anything."

"I'd appreciate that," Cissy said, thinking of her dwindling resources. Except for several stacks of cash bruising her hip. "Any idea?"

Al studied the car like an artist before a canvas. "Considering the car's year, depends on whether I can find the replacement parts at one of the junkyards. I'll give you a break of course, being you're a friend of Nick's."

"When do you think I could get her back?"

"Let's see." He looked over the lot. "Provided my wife's good-for-nothing nephew shows up at a decent hour tomorrow, and, like I said, I can find the parts, and I don't have too much trouble matching the paint—you know who painted her?"

Cissy shook her head. "I could ask my stepfather." She dreaded having to tell Eddie she had been in an accident with the Thunderbird and his insurance premiums would be going up.

Al shrugged, lit a cigarette. "If you find out, give me a call. Otherwise I'll try to match her with the custom charts. Probably won't have her finished for a few days though."

"If there's any way you could have her done sooner, I'd appreciate it."

Al chewed on his cigarette. "Maybe you would, but my other customers might not be so happy."

"I understand." Cissy handed him the keys that had been left in the ignition and followed the two men into the garage to give Al her phone number.

She turned to Nick as they left the garage and walked toward his car. "So, on to the bar."

His expression told her he wasn't buying it. "You've got two choices," he told her as they pulled away from Al's. "Either you choose where you're going to stay or I do."

"Tough guy, huh?" she did in her best James Cagney. "C'mon. I'll buy you a drink."

"I'm still on duty."

"Until when?"

He glanced at his watch. "Another hour."

"You can buy me a drink."

His jaw tightened. She was getting under his skin.

"What's it going to be? The Americana? Omni? Marriott?"

If he thought she was giving up that easily, the man had a short-term memory problem. "Pull over, and drop me off. I'll take a taxi to Fat Eddie's."

He threw her a long look.

"You don't scare me, Fiore. Pull over. I'm not going to sit around in some hotel room when I could be doing something to find my mother and Jo Jo. Besides I've got to tell Eddie about the accident."

"You can call him."

"I'm in the mood for a little social interaction. There's a cab at the corner up there. Pull over."

He swore. She won. She smiled until they drove up to Fat Eddie's. They circled the block until they found parking several side streets down. The new night was no less hot than the day, promising only to get worse before better. The doors to the bar were closed, the air conditioner humming and dripping out a side window. The rest of the windows were dark,

favoring the patrons inside. Music and voices loud-
ened by drink and gregariousness greeted Nick and
Cissy before they even opened the door. Like all tav-
erns, Fat Eddie's had its regulars that paid the bills,
but it also had its curiosity seekers—the newly
twenty-one, the grad students from the nearby uni-
versities. But mainly it was a workingman's bar. No
blender drinks or blue martinis here. The top choice
of drinks was American-brewed beer straight from the
tap, shots and more beer.

Only those sitting nearest to the door glanced up
as Nick and Cissy entered. If any of the faces were
familiar, Cissy didn't recognize them. She scanned
the room, noting interest in several of the women's
faces as they appraised Nick.

There were no stools at the bar. A table would have
seemed too intimate, so they stood, leaning against
the bar's wood edge. Cissy propped one foot jauntily
on the foot-high platform that ran around the bottom
of the bar, clutched her purse to her side and looked
for Eddie. He wasn't behind the bar, where a thick-
waisted man in his mid-thirties with long sideburns
and a brunette with wide but pleasing hips and too
much blue eye shadow poured drafts with little foam.

Sideburns came over to them, but not right away.
It was the hour when the after-work crowd, having
come in for one or two, find they've missed dinner
and oh what the hell, work sucks and the world sucks
and the old lady hadn't wanted to do it since Nixon
and a bar stool never seemed so comfortable. They
had just been joined by those who came much later

but with one purpose—to drink. The combustible combination of the two crowds could result in a brawl or a ball, and Sideburns and Blue Shadow were the ringmasters.

Several minutes went by before either bartender noticed Cissy and Nick. As Sideburns approached, Cissy saw wariness in his eyes as he looked at Nick. Before he could ask "What'll you have?" Nick asked, "Eddie in the back?"

The bartender's wariness increased. "Who's asking?"

Nick jabbed a thumb at Cissy. "His stepdaughter." He met the bartender's watchful gaze as he pulled his badge out. "And Detective Fiore."

The bartender wiped a spot on the bar, unimpressed. "Eddie's not here."

Cissy looked at Nick. His stare stayed on the bartender. "Where can we find him?"

"Did Eddie call?" the bartender yelled to the other bartender. The woman paused in the middle of drawing a draft and shook her head. She set the beer before a pockmarked man and came toward Cissy and Nick, wiping her hands on a dish towel.

"You're looking for Eddie? He called me this morning, asked me if I wanted to pick up an extra shift. I said sure. He said he'd be in the usual time."

"What's the 'usual' time?" Nick asked.

"Usually he's here by six-thirty." The woman glanced at her wristwatch. "Something must have come up."

"He often come in late?"

The woman looked at her co-worker, wondering if she should talk or not.

"He's a cop. She's Eddie's stepdaughter."

"Oh." The woman wrung the towel and looked at Cissy. She held out a hand with a silver pinky ring. "I'm Pauline. I know your mother. Actually, she's been working the Thursday shift for the past few months. Eddie called this morning and asked if I could cover."

"He say why?" Nick asked.

"Nope. And I didn't ask. If the boss's wife wants to take a night off, I figure it's none of my business."

"You try calling Eddie?" Nick asked both of them.

"He's the boss. He calls and checks on us. We don't call him unless there's a problem." The man glanced toward the other side of the bar where someone must have called his name. He nodded. "Which so far this night, there hasn't been. 'Scuse me." He moved away.

"You guys want a drink?" Pauline asked. Nick and Cissy shook their heads.

"You friends with my mother?" Cissy asked.

"We go our separate ways outside of work, but we get along just fine working together. I like your mom. She can make me laugh. She's all right."

"How'd she get along with Eddie?" Nick asked.

Pauline's gaze darted back and forth between Cissy and Nick. "Why?"

"Eddie says she took some cash and her stuff and left him last night."

Pauline looked at Cissy, back to Nick.

"She ever say anything to you about leaving Eddie?"

"She'd moan and groan about her old man like we all do, but leave him? I never heard her say anything like that. They'd just gotten that house. She talked about it all the time. All the things she was going to do to fix it up. She was working extra shifts for the cash."

Cissy felt the weight in her purse. It was more than four nights a week of bar tips.

"So he didn't say anything to you about her taking off on him?"

"When Eddie called this morning, I just figured Louisa needed a night off. Then again, I don't know many men who'd be happy to admit they'd been dumped."

"If that's what happened," Cissy said. Pauline held her gaze. "My stepfather has a temper."

"Well, yeah." Pauline's gaze bounced away. A couple sitting three stools down pushed their glasses to the edge of the bar. Pauline signaled she'd be there in a minute. "I heard the stories. Not from your mother, but some of the other girls." She looked apologetically at Cissy. "Big city. Small talk. But you don't think…" Alarm moved into her heavily made-up features.

"I'm just trying to find out what happened to my mother," Cissy told her.

The woman's expression turned sympathetic. "I wish I could help you. She was all right, your mother.'' The towel tightened in her hands. ''Listen, I gotta get back to work.''

''What about Louisa's other daughter, Jo Jo?'' Nick asked. ''You know her?''

The woman's expression changed. ''Yeah, she comes in now and then.''

''When's the last time you saw her?'' asked Nick.

''She was here a few night ago.'' Pauline glanced at Cissy.

''You can tell me very little that I don't already know about my sister,'' Cissy assured her.

''She wanted money. Your mother was working. She wouldn't give her any, told her if she needed groceries, she'd take her shopping. A bill paid, bring it to her and she'd send a check out. But she wasn't giving her cash. Jo Jo came in last night. Your mother wasn't working, but Eddie was here. This time she wanted to borrow the car.''

''Eddie's car?'' Cissy asked.

''No, the night before Eddie had had a few, so Louisa drove them both home in her car. Eddie drove your mother's car in the next day.''

''The Thunderbird?'' Cissy asked.

Pauline nodded.

''He let Jo Jo take it?'' Nick asked.

''Yeah.''

''She bring it back?'' Nick asked.

''No. Eddie drove his own car home. I figured Jo Jo drove the Thunderbird back to your mom's place.''

Cissy looked at Nick.

"What about Jo Jo's boyfriend? Jacques Saint-Sault? You know him?" Nick continued.

"He came in here once or twice, but not with your sister. He wasn't around much except when his ship docked. Louisa didn't like him, and Louisa liked most people. But she said this guy was no good for Jo Jo. She said Jo Jo had told her about another guy she met, nice guy, steady job, although I never saw him in here with her. Louisa had her fingers crossed this would be the one, the one that would help Jo Jo straighten out her life, you know. I tried to tell her it ain't that simple." She looked at Cissy. "My ex-husband was into the dope." She looked away, her face closed.

"Louisa ever mention this other guy's name?" Nick asked.

Pauline shook her head. "I don't think Louisa knew. Who knows? Jo Jo could have made him up. The gal was prone to flights of fancy, if you know what I mean."

"Eddie keep a gun around?" Nick asked. "For protection?"

"He did."

"He did?"

"Somebody snatched it a couple of weeks ago. He filed a report with the police."

Nick slid a card across the bar. "If you think of anything else, here's my number."

The woman tucked the card in her back pocket. Cissy took out a pen, wrote a phone number on a cocktail napkin.

''This is my cell number. If you hear from my mother or Jo Jo, would you give it to them?''

The woman took the napkin. ''Sure I can't get you guys anything?''

Cissy shook her head.

''When your partner has a minute, I'd like to talk to him,'' Nick said. Pauline nodded and headed to the other end of the bar.

''Jo Jo had the Thunderbird. She must have been the last one to drive it.''

''Perhaps,'' was all Nick would give up.

Cissy watched the woman. ''Kind of convenient Eddie's gun was stolen, don't you think?''

''It happens.'' If Nick suspected anything, he wasn't sharing it with her.

She reached into her purse, past the cash, pulled out her cell phone. ''I'm going to call the house, see if Eddie's there.'' After four rings, the answering machine clicked on. She closed her eyes as her mother's recorded voice told the caller to leave a message. Would it be the last thing she'd ever hear her mother say? She opened her eyes. Nick was watching her. She erased any expression, held his gaze as she asked Eddie or anyone for that matter to pick up if they were there. She waited a few seconds, left her cell phone number and told Eddie to call her. She disconnected, dropped the phone back into her purse. Nick's gaze stayed on her.

''I got the answering machine. My mother's voice was on the message.'' Nick was kind enough not to show sympathy.

The other bartender came up to them. "Pauline said you wanted to see me?"

"I've got just a few questions. Did Eddie ever talk to you about his marriage?"

The man held up his hands. "I come here, do my job. I don't get involved in nobody's personal business."

"So, you and Eddie, you never talked?"

"Sure, we talked. Just not about his marriage. Eddie is the boss."

"What about Louisa?"

"She's the boss's wife."

"What about Jo Jo Spagnola? You know her?"

"Sure, I know her. She's Eddie's stepdaughter. She comes in now and then."

"Seen her lately?"

"Nope."

"Pauline said she was in last night."

"I was off last night."

"Said she was in the night before, too."

The man's gaze held steady, but his pupils danced. "I must have missed her."

"What about her boyfriend, Jacques Saint-Sault? Works the boats. You know him?"

"Nope."

"Work here long?"

"About three months."

"Got a name?"

"Manny Keenan."

Nick pulled out a card. "Just in case something jogs your memory, Manny."

The bartender reached for the card. Tattooed on his inner forearm was an upside-down cross.

"You a member of the Lords, Manny?"

"That's right."

"You own a black Harley?"

"Silver." He glanced down the bar. "We finished here?"

"If Eddie comes in, tell him we'd like to talk to him."

The bartender nodded, moved off toward another customer.

"He's lying about something," Cissy said as they left the bar.

"Not about the Harley." Parked in the alley beside the bar was a silver motorcycle.

"No, it wasn't him who threatened me earlier."

Nick sent her a sharp look.

"The man on the motorcycle this afternoon was much smaller. I thought the feds broke up the Lords in that bust back in the eighties," she said, changing the subject. Eddie's own son from his first wife had been a member of the motorcycle gang. His trial had been coming up when he'd been fatally stabbed in a bar fight over an ex-girlfriend.

"They did."

Behind Nick's beautiful dark eyes she saw his wheels spinning. Whatever he was thinking, though, he wasn't going to share it with her. She opened the car door, and her purse banged against her side. Everybody had their secrets.

"A lot of them served out their sentences and have

been released the past few years. Enough to set up a clubhouse and a grocery-store operation over on Third Avenue. So far, they've kept a low profile.''

"You think the Lords have something to do with my mother and Jo Jo's disappearance?"

"One of their members is working at the bar."

"And Eddie's son was a member."

Nick started up the car. "That firebombing that killed my cousin. The bar's owner was a rival of Eddie's. No evidence was ever found, but word was Eddie's son and his buddies were behind the bombing.''

She put her hand on his, gazed at his hard profile, but knew enough not to say anything.

Nick drove, watching the street. "You need to get a room.''

"Okay.''

The glance he shot her said he'd been expecting an argument. Her compliance was equally suspect. Hard man to please.

"Where to?" Nick headed the car uptown. "Americana? The Towers?"

Cissy thought of her depleting resources. "Didn't we pass the Bel-Air on the way over?"

Nick sent her another look. "What are you doing? Trying to relive your misspent youth?"

She hadn't remembered until Nick's remark that the Bel-Air Motor Lodge had rented rooms by the hour, earning it the nickname the Make-Out Motor Lodge from the high school students who frequented it.

"No, trying to relive yours."

He cracked a grin, completely shameless.

"Okay." He swung into the outer lane. "The Bel-Air it is."

Several minutes later he pulled into the parking lot.

"You have my number?" She stalled. It was easy to play big and bad when cruising around with an Italian hard body with a mean-streets attitude and a fully licensed weapon. She looked at the Vacancy swinging beneath the motel's sign. Story of her life, she thought.

Nick eyed her with a narrow gaze. "Let me take you to my sister's. You remember Mary Theresa. She married a lawyer. A good guy. She's got a Colonial in a ritzy development outside the city. Keeps popping out kids and making Mama happy."

He was stalling, too, Cissy realized. A puppy-dog warmth spread through her limbs. She leaned over and kissed him on the mouth midsentence. It wasn't the smartest thing she'd ever done, but as her lips met his, tasting his own sweet shock, it was the most satisfying.

She let it ride, lingering, as their lips clung. Her mouth relaxed as if to sigh, as if it'd been searching a long time for something, someone to take away the hunger. Her mind marveled that in all these years she hadn't realized she'd already found it. She'd sworn she'd forgotten him. She'd lied.

She knew she'd have to be the first to pull away. To begin with, there was the male maxim that said a woman kisses you, you kiss back—hard. Second, she'd initiated the action; it was up to her to end it. Another unwritten code of sexual conduct.

She knew all this, but she did nothing about it except lean deeper into the kiss, letting all else go and listen to the purr build into a roar. She lengthened her tongue, loosened her lips and took from Nick the one thing he was so willing to share. Damn generous. Damn good.

Of course, like any proper Catholic girl, even the blood rushing to all her sensitive parts and the drunken wash of desire couldn't block out her mother's voice warning what happens to bad girls who neck in boys' cars. Firmly etched in her universal Catholic consciousness were her mother's dire prophesies about boys and back seats, even though Cissy strongly suspected it was how she herself came to be.

Still, it wasn't her mother's cautions that caused her to push away, hadn't been for a long time. It was her mother's disappearance and a million more questions concerning the mystery.

She drew back, her arm wrapped round Nick's neck, her other hand tight to his bicep. She pulled away slowly.

"Did we just break some sort of law here or something?" Ah, she liked the glaze in his eyes. One blink and it was back to the edgy stare, Nick-style. God bless. Gone was the man who'd had his socks rocked, but she'd seen him, confirming what she'd always suspected. Nick Fiore had a heart. He just preferred to keep it hidden beneath a body built for pleasure and an A-1 bad-ass manner. She didn't blame him one bit.

"Not unless I missed something," he answered with his bad-guy grin.

She smiled back. *I'm on to you, Fiore.* "So, making out in a law-enforcement vehicle? That's not violating some kind of statute or something?"

"I've never seen anything about it in the code book."

She deliberately said nothing, staring him down, giving him the chance to grab her—or maybe she'd grab him again. He was the first to look away. She'd won. He was scared. Scared as she. Or he would have wrapped his hand around the back of her head and dragged her to him and not cared less.

She leaned over, whispered in his ear, "You're going down for the count this time, Fiore."

She slid across the seat, opened the door, and almost made it out when his hand caught her upper arm and pulled her back onto his lap, the steering wheel pressing into the back of her head and his mouth moving into hers without retreat. For several minutes, he kissed and coaxed and nipped and stroked her until her nails dug into his shoulders and her hips pressed to him, her entire body thrusting forward as if having discovered a new natural law of physics. He didn't let up. No let up at all, and what a fine thing it was.

He stopped as he'd started, looked down at her, the conqueror in his eyes. She leaned her head on the steering wheel, a violence between them. Cut from the same cloth, they'd either kill each other or love each other like no other. Either way, they were doomed.

"If I go down," he said, "you're going with me."

It was the best offer she'd had in a lifetime. She slid out the door, grabbed her bag from the back seat, propped her arm on the opened door and leaned into the car. "You'll let me know if you get anything from Eddie."

"What are we? Partners now?"

"That's right. Call me." She slammed the door and walked to the motel office, giving him her best backside show. She didn't turn and look as she heard the car shift into reverse, roll out of the parking lot. If she were sixteen again, and he was seventeen, he would gun the engine and peel out. But she wasn't sixteen. He wasn't seventeen. She was thirty-two with a missing mother and sister and only a month of severance between her and the streets. He was thirty-three, a detective who had seen human depravity in all its many incarnations. Still, she'd bet her last year of decent dividends as he eased the unmarked vehicle into traffic and pulled smoothly away, he was smiling. Just like her.

Chapter Five

The two-story house with Victorian flourishes was part of a sprawling residential development named Grandview Estates, in the hope of distinguishing it from the numerous other developments that sprouted like goosegrass twenty minutes from easy access to the interstate. The houses were moderate Capes, long ranches, with the occasional brick front and thirty-three thousand interior thrown in. Cissy drove slowly past number eighteen in her rented Buick. The house was cream; its trim, white. The yard was tidy, the walk trimmed with lush hosta, the flower beds beneath the half porch's rail bursting with petunias and pansies. Certainly not Cissy's idea of a killer's lair. Then again, motorcycle-riding, gun-wielding maniacs didn't usually dress in Botany 500 either.

She drove several blocks over, the deepening night dark enough for her to turn her headlights on. Several people were still out walking, most with dogs. Children splashed and yelled in a pool. Balls and swing sets littered the yards. Many waved as she passed despite the fact that they didn't recognize the car. Nothing like suburbia to bring a lump to your throat.

Cissy circled, came back toward number eighteen. What was the plan here? She couldn't just walk up and ask, "Excuse me? Did you try to off me today at the corner of Manning and Maiden?"

She parked at the far edge of the lawn, not wanting to circle a third time. She'd already seen some of the welcoming looks turn curious. Suspicion was next. Suburbia was sweet but it wasn't stupid.

She rolled down the window and stared at the house and its example of everything true and pure and great about America. Maybe Nick was right. Maybe she was overreacting. Maybe what she thought was a gun had been the sun's glare, a reflection off the metal handle bars, an illusion from the mirror's refractory rays or simple female hysteria. She closed her eyes, again pictured the motorcycle, the man and saw the gun again as clear as holy water. The son of a bitch had tried to kill her.

"Can I help you?"

She gave a squeak, her eyes flying open. An elderly woman, her light blue eyes and features gone from pretty to kindly by way of numerous wrinkles, stood small but sturdy-looking in her Reeboks and culottes and canvas fisherman's hat. "I didn't mean to startle you."

"I'm looking for Phillip Lester's house."

"You found it. Right on the money." The woman's face folded up within itself more as she smiled and gestured to the cream ranch with the white trim. "Such a nice young man. Keeps a nice place too, don't you think? Don't know if he's home, though."

The house did look dark. The garage doors were down. "Maybe I missed him. I'll just go and ring the bell to make sure. Have a good night now." Cissy attempted to get the woman moving on her way. She got out of the car and started up the drive, a queasy sensation in her stomach, like the time in college when she'd washed down guacamole and tortilla chips with several pints of dark beer. Well, if ol' Phil was home and answered the door, he certainly wouldn't kill her on his front porch, she reasoned. Not with all the cream and white and weedless flower beds.

She rang the bell, waited, waved to the elderly lady who had turned the corner and was continuing up the street parallel to Lester's house. No answer. No sound of life inside. At least she'd tried. She turned to go, met the black garage door windows. She stepped off the porch, strolled to the drive, looking up and down the streets. The mother across the street was busy shrieking at the children in the pool. A jogger going by was focusing in front of him, probably trying to envision the end of his self-imposed torture. Cissy cupped her hands and peered through the dark squares into the garage.

Centered in one half of the cement floor, black and arrogantly shiny even in the gloom was a Harley-Davidson motorcycle. A satisfied smile came to Cissy's face. She peered harder as if expecting to find an answer. Nothing. The garage was as neat as the house's exterior.

She stepped back, studied the house. Imagined the inside reflected it's owner's fastidiousness. Not the type of person to chase a woman in broad daylight and attempt to shoot her on one of the city's busiest corners.

She stared at the house. Was the answer inside? Had this man of the monster motorcycle and the tended flower gardens tried to kill her? Did he know what had happened to her mother and sister?

She circled the garage to the back door, knocked again. Hard. Still no answer. She fumbled through her purse for a safety pin, bent it open, shaped the tip, inserted it into the lock and jiggled, a technique everybody had known back in the neighborhood but she hadn't employed since returning from a midnight rendezvous at sixteen and finding the front door locked, the key under the mat removed by her mother.

Five minutes later, she heard a click, opened the door. No chain and bolt. Nice neighborhood. She stepped into the kitchen, more than the air-conditioning going full force making her shiver. Technically she wasn't doing anything wrong, she told herself as she scanned the room. She wasn't going to take anything. Just look for something, anything that might help her find her mother and sister.

She shut the door. Plus the man had tried to shoot her. Justification enough for her to tiptoe across his linoleum. She crept into the hall, staying close to the wall in her best emulation of every Dirty Harry movie she'd ever seen. She poked her head around the corner, then drew back again. Slower this time, she peeked, her back pressed to the wall. A typical living room with the customary couch, early Colonial style, blue-and-red plaid. A chair and ottoman, the same shade of blue as in the couch, were nearby. Two maple tray tables with elegant legs served as a coffee table. Phil Lester had better taste than most men Cissy had known. She moved down to a room set up as an office with a variety of computer equipment. Most men loved the gadgets and gizmos of this age, taking a primitive pride in the size of their RAM and hard drive. Phil was obviously one of the ranks. She stepped into the room. A changing multicolored shape swam in and out of the twenty-one inch monitor screen. She looked around, pressed a button on the keyboard. Program icons in even rows filled the screen. Cissy read the names. Many were typical software needed for personal computers. Others were unfamiliar to Cissy, but from the icons and their names, most seemed to be some kind of game. All this told her was Phil was a gamer. Not a killer.

She sighed a deep supersleuth sigh and tried to think like Nancy Drew. When that produced nothing, she climbed the stairs. At the top to her left was what appeared to be a spare bedroom. Directly in front was a bathroom and to her right, what had to be Phil's bedroom, with its masculine hunter green colors and vertical blinds across the windows. She walked into the bathroom. Freud, Jung and others had their theories on personality but Cissy believed the essence of a man lay behind two doors—his refrigerator's and his bathroom medicine cabinet's. She slid back one mirrored door on the cabinet over the sink. After-shave, razors, aspirin, toothpaste, mouthwash, dental floss. Phil followed an excellent hygienic routine. She had not expected otherwise. She slid the mirrored panel closed and slid over the other one.

Several bottles of different types of antacid in var-ying colors and sizes sat on the clean glass shelves. Two prescription bottles, half-filled, sat on the shelves. Cissy turned their labels toward her. Nexium. Prilosec. Medicine prescribed to counteract nervous stomachs. Two-thirds of the brokers Cissy had known had popped them daily. She moved to the bedroom, faced the tall dresser on the opposite wall. She wasn't really going to go through his drawers, was she? Okay, the man had tried to shoot her but something about rifling through his skivvies seemed very un-Nancy Drew-like. She darted her gaze around the room, hoping for deliverance. Several books were stacked evenly on the bottom shelf of the nightstand. A clock-radio and telephone sat on top beside a read-ing lamp. Her gaze swung to the closet. She moved toward it in the gathering dusk, trying not to let the shadows spook her.

She pushed back the sliding door. It stuck halfway. She pushed harder when a ringing made her jump. She glanced wildly around, her heart banging against her chest. Realizing it was her cell phone did nothing to spell the hammering of her heart. She groped in her purse, sweat trickling under her armpits. Nancy

Drew would have turned her cell off. The ringing continued persistent as a mother's guilt. Oh, screw Nancy Drew. Cissy dumped her purse on Phil's bounce-a-quarter-off-it bed and grabbed her phone. She jabbed Talk. "What?"

"Where the hell are you?"

Nick. "Why don't you strap me with one of those electronic ankle bracelets and we can skip the formalities." Propping the phone on her shoulder, she scrambled to shove everything back in her purse, including the two stacks of cash that she still didn't know what to do with but couldn't leave in the motel room.

"A call came in from Standish Security. A silent alarm was triggered at Eighteen Pleasant Pond Drive."

Uh-oh.

"Get the hell out of there."

The line went dead. For once she'd do what she was told.

Her purse tucked under her arm, she ran down the stairs without a plan. She froze, pulled up flat against the wall as headlights swept the room. A car pulled into the driveway. She heard the whir of the garage door opening. Lester. Most likely, he would come in through the back door. On her hands and knees, she crawled past the side windows toward the front door. Still on her knees, she reached up, unlocked the front door, wincing at the click. She pressed on the handle, inch by silent inch swung the door open. Only then did she straighten up and step out into the hot night, pulling the door carefully closed behind her. She tensed every muscle as she waited for the final click. She released her breath, turned.

"Hi, honey."

Coming toward her up the stairs was a medium-built man with dark hair and a mean smile. Past the man's shoulder she saw a patrol car come down the street. It slowed, pulled into the drive, its headlights sweeping the front yard.

She was enveloped in a bone-crunching hug. The man's arm slithered down her side to pull up his loose-fitting shirt, slip out the gun in his waistband, press its snout to her navel. "Don't give me any problems," he muttered.

She had finally met Phillip Lester.

Chapter Six

"What's your name?" the man growled in her ear.

"Candy," Cissy lied.

Two uniformed cops got out of the car. Her captor flattened his lips against hers as he pressed the gun deeper into her belly's soft flesh. She found his lower lip, pulled it into her mouth, heard his delighted moan and bit down hard.

He snapped his head back. *Go for it,* her gaze openly challenged him. If she was going to die, it wasn't going to be without a fight.

His back to the police and several curious neighbors looking on from their yards, he glared at her as he cocked the gun's trigger.

Cissy rolled her eyes. "Shoot me while the police and the neighborhood watches. See how many barbecues you'll be invited to next summer."

Her captor moved around to her backside and nestled the gun in her spine as the police came up the drive. "No more fooling around. Smile."

Cissy's lips curved. She thought she would throw up.

"Sorry to bring you out here like this, Officers. I was expecting my friend Candy here, but had to go out. Work emergency." He sighed. "Never ends, does it? Anyway, I couldn't get her on her cell." He turned to her. "Honey, I've told you a million times, it doesn't work unless you turn it on."

The point of the gun burrowed into her back.

"I'm such a ditz." She forced a strained giggle.

"But I love her anyway." He nuzzled her neck. She swallowed down the bile rising into her mouth.

"So I left her a note. Told her to let herself in with her key, but of course she didn't think about the alarm. Again." He added a note of amused tolerance. "Sorry for the false alarm, Officers."

"In the future, try to remember to deactivate the alarm, ma'am," said one of the cops.

The man nudged her with the gun barrel.

"Yes, sir." Her voice cracked. The gun dug into her spine. "Thank you, Officers."

Lester kept her pinned against him as the officers walked back to their vehicle and got in. The patrol car pulled out of the drive. With her body still pressed tightly against his, Lester turned them both to the door. He flattened her body against it. "Open it."

She didn't have a chance if she let him get her alone. She pretended to press on the handle, wiggled it. "It must have locked automatically."

The man reached past her to the door. Cissy held her breath. He pressed on the latch, pushed, swore. The door *had* locked automatically. Cissy smelled her own perspiration and the stronger, sour smell of the man's sweat.

"Okay, we're gonna walk down the porch." He turned her around. "Put your arm around my waist."

She did as he said. The man put his arm around her shoulders, clasping her tight to his side, the gun in her rib cage. "That's it. Nice and easy." They moved together down the porch.

"Why'd you try and kill me this afternoon?"

The man looked at her, released a laugh. "I didn't try and kill you…yet. Come on. We're going to the garage. Take a ride."

Cissy stumbled, hoping to break his hold, make a run for it. The man clamped his arm on her shoulder, jerking her upright. He shoved the gun deeper into her ribs.

"On the Harley?" she asked. "The same Harley you were riding when you tried to shoot me downtown this afternoon?"

"If I took a shot at you, you'd be dead."

"But it *was* you on the Harley today, wasn't it? Why do you want to kill me?"

He pushed her into the garage, aimed the gun at her. "You tell me—what were you doing in the house? What were you looking for?"

"I just told you 'somebody'—" she made quotation marks with her fingers "—on that motorcycle pulled up beside me and aimed a gun at me." She looked down the gun barrel. "Twice in one day. What are the odds?"

"How do you know it was that motorcycle?"

"I got a number and two letters of the license plate number, found out who it was registered to, came over here tonight to find out why you were chasing me today. You weren't home." She shrugged. "I decided to have a look around myself."

"Find anything interesting?"

"You're a little bit on the obsessive-compulsive side."

He motioned with the gun toward the compact Hyundai. "Get in the car."

"Where's my mother? And my sister? You don't look like the type to hang out with Eddie Vitelli, but then again, crime makes for strange bedfellows."

He started toward her. She backed away but kept her voice fierce.

"I want to know what happened to them. Louisa Vitelli. Jo Jo Spagnola."

He was almost to her when they both heard a loud knocking close to the garage.

"Mr. Lester, this is the police again." The knocking stopped. Footsteps moved toward the back, then stopped when they saw the sliver of light under the garage door. "Mr. Lester?"

The man grabbed Cissy's arm, pulled her toward the door, the gun against her temple.

"We'll be right out, Officer. We're in the garage here and...give us a minute, would you? We're in a rather delicate situation, if you know what I mean." He gave a suggestive laugh. Cissy stuck her finger down her throat.

The officer outside the door chuckled, man to man.

"That's all right. I actually only had one last question."

"Shoot." Lester smiled a sickly grin at her.

"Who the hell is Candy?" The door was kicked in, slamming into Lester. Cissy broke free as he was thrown against the motorcycle. She grabbed a thick-headed driver from the bag of golf clubs, spun and struck him on the back of the head. The gun flew out of his hand, went off as the motorcycle toppled to its side. Lester sprawled across it, knocked out cold.

Panting, holding the golf club high as if to strike again, Cissy looked up into Nick's pissed-off gaze. His weapon on the man, he bent down and picked up the other gun. He stood, one gun aimed, the other ready at his side. She didn't stand a chance.

She dropped the golf club, let it clatter against the cement floor. She walked toward Nick, everything inside her crumbling. She stopped inches from him, looked up into those angry, scared eyes and knew the feeling. First time in her life she'd ever seen fear on Fiore's fine face. She reached a hand to his rough cheek. "I'm sorry." She meant it. To scare Fiore was a sin.

She dropped her hand. "You didn't know I played golf, did you?"

Her forehead fell to his chest. She closed her eyes against any tears and leaned into the sure strength of him.

A gun still tight in his hand, he wrapped his arm around her bowed head.

"Is everything all right?" A voice came from the door.

Cissy and Nick broke apart. A stout man in a bathing suit stood at the doorway.

"I live two houses over," the man provided. "I was getting out of the pool when I thought I heard a gunshot."

Nick pulled out his shield. "Detective Fiore. Everything's under control."

Atop the bike, Lester started to stir.

"Have you noticed any suspicious activity around here recently, Mr....?" Nick waited for the neighbor to fill in the blank.

"Roth. Wayne Roth." He stepped inside the garage, stuck out his hand. "No, this is a quiet neighborhood. Young families. Retirees. The most excitement I can remember around here is last summer, when Esther Wills over on Cactus got a karaoke machine and set to practicing Patsy Cline on her screened porch. Even the cats were scared out of the neighborhood."

A low groan came from the man sprawled across the bike.

"What about Lester?" Nick asked the neighbor.

"Phil, he's a good guy. Anytime the Little League or the Soccer Club or the Garden Association needs fliers or signs, Phil prints them up. Quiet fellow. Keeps to himself mostly but like I said, a nice guy.

Lester attempted to rise from the motorcycle.

Gun aimed, Nick walked over to the bike, pulled the man up with one hand. "Nice guy or not, I'm afraid we're going to have to take Phil here down to the station.'' The man stumbled, looked around, dazed. Nick pulled his arms behind his back. ''You have the right—''

''That's not Phil Lester.''

Cissy's and Nick's gazes shot to the neighbor. ''What do you mean?'' Nick asked

The man shook his head. ''That's not Phil Lester.''

Nick and Cissy looked at the handcuffed man.

''I don't say nothing without my lawyer present.'' The man squeezed his eyes shut, moaned.

''Let's go then, kids.'' Nick grabbed the man's arm, gave Cissy a pointed look. ''Ladies first.''

He wasn't taking any more chances, Cissy realized. After this, he'd be on her worse than a parolee freshly sprung. The fact the idea wasn't exactly unappealing distressed her even more.

''Mr. Roth?'' Nick handed the neighbor his card. ''If you or anyone else in the neighborhood happens to see Mr. Lester or has any information concerning him, I'd appreciate a call.''

''Of course. You don't think something has happened to Phil, do you?'' He eyed the handcuffed man. ''Who's this guy anyway?''

Nick pushed the handcuffed man out the garage door, snapped off the light. ''That's what I'm going to find out.''

CISSY WAITED in the station breakroom, a can of soda sweating on the table in front of her. Periodically she reminded herself to breathe when her surroundings began to blur at the edges. Nick finished and found her staring at the revolving microwave burgers and Hostess apple pies. ''Hey,'' he said softly as if not to startle her. ''Ready?'' She reminded herself once more to breathe and stood.

Earlier Nick had showered at the station, changed into cotton pants and a Packers T-shirt. He'd had the Harley's partial plate numbers run, gotten Lester's address and breezed by his place this afternoon after he'd dropped Cissy off at the DMV. No one had been home. After he'd brought Cissy to the motel, he'd stopped by the station to finish up the day's paperwork and sign out before he made another visit to Lester's. He'd been heading there when he'd heard the dispatch to Lester's residence. He'd met the patrol officers on their way out of the development. They'd explained to him it was a false alarm. The resident's bubbleheaded girlfriend named Candy had forgotten to turn off the alarm. Sensing it was a lie, Nick had rushed to Lester's house.

''Bubbleheaded, my butt.''

He stopped, forced her to face him. ''This isn't a game, Cissy. Do you understand that?''

''I know this isn't a game.'' Her voice was quiet, even. ''My mother and sister are missing. I want to know what happened to them.''

Nick sighed, looked weary. ''It's not your fault, Cissy. You're not the guilty one.''

''Can't help it.'' She shrugged. ''It's the Catholic curse.''

He shook his head. No arguing with the Catholic curse. "Come on, let's get you out of here."

They stepped out of the air-conditioned station. The heat slammed into them like a sucker punch.

"So, what did you find out from our Lester impersonator?" Cissy knew he would only tell her the basics. Anything really pertinent to the case wasn't coming from those gorgeous lips. Not to her ears anyway.

"Guy's name is Steve Deed. Claims he's a friend of Lester's, staying there a few days. Claims Lester let him borrow the car. Lester had the bike. Came home, house was empty, figured Lester was working late, so he went out for a few drinks."

"Yeah, right." Cissy kicked a piece of gravel.

"Another detective recognized him. Said they brought him in a few years ago on the Gambino brothers' bust. They used to run the books on the northside. Stevie did their dirty work. 'Stevie the Sledgehammer' was his name on the street. That's who you were dancing with tonight."

He was waiting for a reaction from her. He wasn't going to get it.

"Vice says they haven't seen Stevie in a while. Not since the Gambino brothers went under. Figured he left the area, on to greener pastures."

"So where's Phil Lester?" And her mother? And her sister?

"Stevie wasn't talking. Made a call and a high-priced mouthpiece, a real hotshot, was here within the hour and sprang him. I don't know who he's working for but it's somebody connected."

"He's out already?"

"We couldn't hold him. He had a permit for the .45. Nothing had been taken from the house. Lester can't be found to refute Deed's story or to file charges. We have no proof that he wasn't telling the truth."

"The man shoved a gun in my side and threatened to kill me."

Nick smiled. "Says you broke into the house, which you did. Says you assaulted him. Which you did. From the look of him, he's got the stronger case."

"That was self-defense."

"That's what *he's* claiming. And you did enter the house illegally."

"I knocked."

He rubbed the side of his head.

"I didn't go over there with the intention of picking Lester's lock. I rang the bell, knocked on the door, was going to leave when I saw the Harley in the garage. I don't know. I thought maybe I could find a clue, something, anything that might tell me where Mama and Jo Jo are."

"Listen." He stopped, took her by the shoulders as if to shake her but only held her firm. "You pull a stunt like that again, and I'll handcuff you to my bed."

"You have an unhealthy fixation on handcuffs, you know."

His arms tensed as if straining not to shake her. She'd seen he'd been scared back there. Scared for her.

He didn't like it. Neither did she. Start to care, and you lose your edge. Start to feel, and you lose your head.

"All right." She shrugged out of his hold. "I'll be a good girl."

He pulled her to him as if fighting it all the way, but his kiss was urgent and hard and made her knees bend. It was the leftover fear they were trying to purge. That combined with the gathering sexual swelter between them.

He pulled away. "You don't have to go that far," he whispered against her ear. The fear may have been temporarily quelled but the desire between them was reaching new degrees. Light a match and they'd both blow. "But let me do my job."

They broke apart, silent until they came to Nick's car. He opened the driver's door. "We'll leave the rental at Lester's tonight. Pick it up tomorrow. I'll take you to the motel so you can get your bag. You'll stay at my place." He rounded the car, not waiting for her answer.

"You're not serious." She looked across the roof of the car, saw he was.

"You're staying with me."

She knew it was the closest he'd admit to how scared he'd been. She didn't protest again. It was the closest she'd admit to how scared she was.

She slid into the car, her legs like lead. She pulled her purse onto her lap, the cash heavy against her thighs.

"Have there been any robberies lately? Maybe banks? Huge sums of cash missing?"

Nick eyeballed her.

She tried to appear blasé which, given the day, was no small feat. "Just shooting in the dark, trying to figure out what happened to my mother and sister. Not to mention how Lester figures in all this. Or where Lester is for that matter."

"Missing Persons ran your mother's vitals and social security numbers. So far, nothing has shown up. No activity on her credit cards, bank transactions. If she did run off like Eddie said, she's making every effort not to be found."

She heard the "if," understood what Nick was saying but wouldn't accept it. "Tell them to look harder."

They pulled into the motel's parking lot. Nick parked, shut off the engine. She gave a quick intake of breath as he reached across her legs to open the glove compartment. He pulled out a handgun that did nothing to allay Cissy's unease. He held out his hand.

"Give me the key."

"Don't you—" She was about to say "just kick the door in?" when she remembered less then two hours ago, that's exactly what he'd done, saving her. She found the key, dropped it into his palm. Even a smartass knew when not to push her luck.

Nick unlocked the door, opened it slowly, his weapon ready. She followed so close behind him she stepped on the heel of his sneaker. A blast of cold air from the air conditioner greeted them, although Cissy could have sworn she had turned the air conditioner almost off when she'd left, fearing the room would be like an icebox when she returned.

Nick found the switch, clicked it on. His body came to full alert. He turned, trying to shield Cissy's view, but not before she thought she saw a figure in the easy chair beside the bed.

"Go outside. Now."

"Who is it?"

"Go outside."

"No." Whatever lay beyond would be worse imagined than the reality. Nick reached for her but she ducked around him into the room. A medium-size balding man was sitting quite comfortably in the armchair, his head resting on its high back. His mouth was parted, the corners drooped, giving his face a disappointed look. His eyes were bloodless and blank, a bullet hole in his forehead. In his lap, leaning against his chest, a cardboard square read Go Home.

She stared until she couldn't take it anymore. Her eyes came up slowly to meet Nick's. His face was washed clean of expression. Depersonalization. A cop's greatest weapon. Her hand was clutching the front of his T-shirt. He covered her fingers with his own, his grasp not gentle.

"Stand outside the door. I'll be right out."

She didn't argue. She stood on the narrow cement strip that ran outside all the ground floor rooms, listening to Nick call the station. She didn't turn when he came out, afraid her eyes would give her away. She stood on the cement, staring out at the white lines of the parking lot. The sweat beaded on her body and trickled into the hollow of her back, along her hairline, between her breasts. Nick stood next to her.

''How long has he been…in there?'' She was not brave in the darkness with death in an armchair steps away.

''Not long. What time did you leave?''

''About eight-thirty.''

''He's been dead longer than that. Somebody must have killed him earlier and brought the body here. Somebody who wanted to scare you.''

It'd worked.

''Who is he?''

''I don't want to disturb anything until Homicide gets here. Your bag is in there. If they were looking for something, they were neat about it. Professional. Nothing seems to be missing. There was no robbery.''

''Just murder.'' Her voice had an offbeat sound. She stepped involuntarily an inch closer to Nick. He put his arm around her shoulders. They were standing that way when the squad car pulled up, followed by an unmarked Chevy.

''Do you want to wait in the car?'' He was being gentle with her. She didn't think she would cry until that moment.

She nodded, walked to the car while Nick met the others. They conferred for a moment at the door's entrance, then followed Nick inside, except for a uniformed officer who came over to interview her. Cissy knew he was also there for her protection. She answered his questions. The motel manager came to the room in a sleeveless T-shirt, the elastic waistband of his cotton shorts stretched tight across his stomach. Another officer knocked on the other room doors, the occupants inside quickly losing the rumpled look of late night when they learned the reason for the disturbance. The attendants from the coroner's office arrived. An empty stretcher was wheeled in, came back out with a bulky black body bag. Cissy pushed open the car door, dashed for the end of the building. At the corner, in the glow of the vending machines, she heaved. She was doubled over, panting, when Nick came up behind her.

She straightened. He put change into the machine, pushed a button, handed her a soda. She pressed the can to her forehead, the side of her neck. He bought another soda, popped it open, took a long drink, watching her.

"Well, there's one question we don't have to ask anymore."

She opened the soda and took a drink, trying to get rid of the aftertaste in her mouth. "What's that?"

"Where's Phillip Lester?"

Chapter Seven

Nick lived on a side street several blocks from downtown in an area known for its trendy shops and funky bars. The buildings lining his street were architecturally impressive, many converted into townhouses, bright with summer flowers potted on their stoops or filling in the three-by-three foot plots behind black iron fences. Nick's building was brick and black-shuttered with no flowers out front. His apartment was a one-bedroom walk-up on the third floor. The ceilings were high, the windows long. Furnishings were the male necessities—couch, recliner, dinette set, everything utilitarian and inexpensive. There were no doilies, matted prints or refrigerator magnets. His kitchen window looked out on the high towers of the projects six blocks away. The only exotic element was a huge fish tank against the living room wall. Cissy walked over to check out the colorful fish. She glanced at Nick over her shoulder.

He shrugged. "You don't have to walk them." He took out two beers from the refrigerator, a bag of chips from the cupboard. He was halfway to the living room when his cell phone rang.

Even with the buzz of the air conditioner Nick had cranked up to high as soon as they'd walked in, there was really no place in the apartment where Cissy couldn't hear his voice. She stepped into the bathroom, ran the water in an attempt to give him privacy. Still she heard ''Uh-huh, yup, okay.'' Nick was a man of action, not words.

She tried not to listen. She was tempted to explore his medicine cabinet but wasn't sure she was ready for what she would learn. Forgoing the spotted glass on the counter, she cupped her hands and drank straight from the faucet, her mouth as dry as the brown fields she'd passed this morning on the way to her mother's house. She spit, the city water leaving a metallic taste in her mouth, wiped her hands on a towel flung over the top of the shower. Her nose and cheeks were slightly sunburned. Tomorrow they would turn brown, primed to wrinkle at an early age. Her hair was limp where sweat and fear had pasted it to her neck. She put the toilet seat and cover down and sat and waited for the call to be finished. Dirty towels were heaped in the corner near the hamper. An opened toothpaste tube lay on the sink counter, several smears of toothpaste in the basin. Cissy resisted the urge to pick up, wipe off. Instead she said, with too much endearment, ''What a slob.''

When she heard nothing but silence for several minutes, she got up and came out of the bathroom, her hands damp.

''As I thought, Lester was killed much earlier, before the body was dumped in your room. They're looking for Deed now.''

''They think he did it?''

''No evidence yet. They couldn't find any prints, but Deed's too smart for that anyway. He probably used Lester's car and was returning from dropping off the body in the motel room when he ran into you. Forensics is going over the car and Lester's house now hoping to find something. Lester wasn't killed with a .45 though.''

''How do you know?''

''A .45 close range would have been messy. From the looks of Lester, it was a smaller caliber. A .22.''

''But why was the body put in my room?''

''If Deed did do it, he was told to by whoever he's working for. And whoever that is, they want you out of the way. They're being polite about it now, but patience isn't a virtue with these people. Who knew you were staying there besides me?''

''I called my mother's house again from the motel, trying to find Eddie, but all I got was the machine. I left my cell number again and the motel number.''

Nick moved toward the coffee table where he'd set down the beers and bag of chips. ''If Eddie's involved in anything, he's only a small fish. Deed doesn't work for small fish. More likely Eddie and Deed are working for the same boss.''

He popped open the beer, moved toward the recliner. Cissy saw her handbag, sitting where she'd dropped it in the chair's seat. She started toward the

chair but not before Nick picked up her purse.
"Whoa." He levered the purse up and down.
"You're going to get a hernia carrying this thing
around."

"Look at me. Just making myself at home. Dropping crap all over the place. I'm sorry." She reached
for the bag.

"What do you keep in here anyway?" Nick still
tested the bag's weight.

"Stacks of cash." She told him the truth.

He smiled, handed her the purse. She sat on the
couch, put the purse on the floor next to her feet, the
cash that she thought was much more than "emergency money" resting on her ankle.

Nick took a smooth sip. "Women and their
purses."

"Men and their remote controls."

He smiled the smile that had defined her puberty.

"So nobody at the motel saw anything?" She di-
verted his attention away from the subject of her
purse, her own attention away from that smile.

"If they did, they're not coming forward. The place
was only about a quarter full."

"What'll happen when you find Deed?"

Nick leaned all the way back in the recliner.
"We'll bring him in, try to scare him if we don't have
anything, but Deed doesn't scare easy. If we don't
have any proof, and he's not biting, we'll only be able
to hold him until his lawyer shows up and lets the
courts know we've got nothing."

Cissy slumped back into the couch.

"Tomorrow I'll find Eddie and have a little talk with him. I'll also talk to Lester's neighbors and co-workers, try to find a connection. A lead. Forget about it, Spagnola."

Her face must have beamed interest.

"You will stay here."

The man would never learn. "And do what?"

"Feed my fish."

At least he didn't threaten her with handcuffs again. They were making progress.

Nick sat up in the recliner, set his beer can on the coffee table, glanced at the other unopened can. "Can I get you something else? There's some iced tea in there, and water."

"No, I'm fine. I don't want anything right now, thanks."

Nick picked up his own can. "Is there anyone your mother was close to at the bar, outside the bar? Any other relatives?"

"Like I said, I haven't been around much. My mother had one sister but she died about ten years ago. Cancer. My aunt had two sons. One lives in California, the other North Carolina. As far as I know she hasn't heard from them except for Christmas cards."

"It couldn't hurt to give them a call," Nick suggested.

"She did mention one woman now and then. She worked at the bar for a time but I don't think she's there anymore. Mama hadn't mentioned her in a while. They used to go shopping, took a bus trip once down to Atlantic City.''

''Remember her name?'' He was all cop now and sexy as hell.

Cissy closed her eyes to concentrate and block out the appealing image of Nick. ''I think it was something like Gina or Tina. Maybe Nina.'' She opened her eyes. ''If I heard it again, it would ring a bell.''

''I'll ask at the bar tomorrow. See if anyone knows anything.'' He set down his beer and stretched. Cissy watched the ripple of muscle, added it to her list of worries.

''You better get some sleep,'' Nick advised. ''I'll take the couch. You can have the bed.''

''I don't want to kick you out of your bed. I'll take the couch.''

''*I'll* take the couch,'' he said again as if the matter were settled.

''You're bossy, Fiore.''

''Comes with the territory.'' He picked up her small suitcase which he'd carried up from his car and walked into the bedroom. ''You'll have to leave the door open for the air-conditioning.''

Somehow the idea of an opened bedroom door in Nick Fiore's apartment was unsettling. But it was either that or heat stroke. She wasn't sure which was the most dangerous.

He brought out bedding for the couch. She took her suitcase and purse into his bedroom. From the suitcase, she got her toothbrush, dental floss, facial cleanser, toner, night cream, eye cream, lip balm and body lotion out of her suitcase. Gathering the various bottles and tubes in her arms, she went into the bathroom. She wasn't sure if all these creams did diddly, but she was in her thirties now and like most things in her life, she couldn't afford to take chances.

She brushed and cleansed and flossed and creamed, the routine providing a small measure of normalcy in a day that was anything but, and from the looks of it was only the beginning of a strange trip down memory and murder lane. She scooped up her toiletries, almost dropping them when she came out to find Nick in only his gym shorts and a body built by God and Nautilus. Nick's left brow lifted as he looked at the variety of creams and lotions and Madison Avenue dreams in her arms. She let pass his smile that said, "Sucker," as he slowly lifted his gaze to hers. Nor did she argue. He was more right than he probably realized. For all her cynical, streetwise pose, she fell too easily for false promises, a weakness that in the past had only led to disaster and sometimes, a black eye. She had to learn to be more careful. No matter the buzzing inside her and the man before her only gym shorts away from naked. Didn't matter what side of the law he was on, Nick Fiore was trouble. And at the moment, her problem box was overflowing.

She dumped the bottles back into the suitcase.

"Will the television bother you?" Nick called from the other room. "They repeat the late-night news after Letterman."

"No." She doubted she would get much sleep tonight anyway. "In fact, I'll watch it with you." Insomnia. The curse of a conscience.

She went back into the living room, sat on the couch, fully dressed. Something about being in Nick's apartment, never mind his bed, in nothing more than pajamas—granted, perfectly respectable cotton pj's that covered all necessary areas—seemed wrong. Her Catholic nature was rising again.

"If you're hungry or thirsty, there's stuff in the refrigerator and cupboards," Nick offered as he clicked the remote.

She shook her head, too keyed up to eat or drink. They watched a commercial for dog food in silence. A blond-bobbed anchorwoman with an earnest expression came on the screen. "Top stories tonight. Body found in barge." The screen shot away to the port. As Nick collapsed the recliner again, Cissy wished she'd chosen the end of the sofa closer to him. With a promise "We'll be back with the full details along with the day's other top stories after this word from our sponsor," the screen cut to a woman shaking clothes into a washing machine. A swear word involuntarily came out of Cissy's mouth. Nick didn't say a word. He got up, stood behind the sofa. She picked up a throw pillow propped against the couch's arm and hugged it against her chest.

The news returned. "*The Lady of Louisiana* was docked yesterday morning in the city's port on its way to Canada when workers started complaining of an odor aboard the ship. Local authorities were called in when further investigation revealed the source of the foul odor was a locked cargo trunk hidden in a section of the ship's ceiling.''

The screen showed a trunk being pried open with crowbars. Cissy squeezed the pillow tighter.

''When authorities opened the trunk, they found the body of a dead man.''

Cissy let out a breath.

''Authorities have not released the victim's name yet, but they did report the victim was a white male, late-twenties, approximately six feet, one hundred and ninety pounds with long blond hair. The victim had been shot once in the middle of the forehead.''

Cissy went cold all over.

''Agents estimate the body had been dead for about twenty-four hours. Based on a tip from an informant, Federal agents raided a sister ship of the *Lady of Louisiana* last month in New Orleans but no illegal contraband was found aboard the ship. The *Lady of Louisiana* is part of a network of ships used to transport cargo into Canada and into international waters.''

Cissy turned and looked at Nick. He was dialing the phone. ''Got any identification on that body found in the port tonight?'' he asked whoever picked up on the other end. ''How 'bout the weapon?''

She got up, walked over to him. He started toward the bedroom, a closed door, a lowered voice. She clutched his arm, shook her head ''no.'' He stared straight at her as if sending her strength. ''Tell them to check out a Canadian who worked the docks. Jacques Saint-Sault.''

She stared at Nick for several motionless seconds.

He stared back, not letting her go. She walked to the couch, bent to pick up the pillow that had fallen from her lap when she stood, but as she leaned over, the dread claimed her so completely she feared she would keep going, sink into a boneless heap on the floor. She clutched the pillow, straightened with the will that had taken her far from her beginnings and brought her back again.

Nick sat down, fingers loosely laced, hands hanging between his spread knees in an almost *Father Knows Best* pose. "It's a long shot, Cissy."

Neither believed it. She looked into her ex-lover's eyes, seeing the steely determination she wished for herself. "They're dead, aren't they?" she asked in a tinny tone. "My mother and sister. They're dead."

"We don't know that. We've got no evidence. This could be something totally unrelated. The docks aren't a playground. Right now we have an unidentified body on a barge. Nothing else."

"What about the weapon?"

"They're investigating."

"My mother and sister are missing. Meanwhile, corpses are coming out of the woodwork."

"Your mom and Jo Jo could be hiding. Maybe they're involved somehow in whatever is going on. Maybe they know something, saw something. Maybe somebody warned them to lie low for a while because things were heating up."

She wanted to believe him. "There was that one call from Jo Jo."

"What about that phone call you got today?"

"'Go home,'" Cissy remembered.

"You said the voice was disguised. Whoever it was didn't want to be identified. Maybe your sister and mother can't reach you. It's too risky, so they had someone else contact you, warn you."

"Scare me is more like it."

"Maybe your mother and Jo Jo are trying to get you out of town. Afraid you might get hurt."

"Well, somebody sure as hell doesn't want me around. The corpse-a-gram in my motel room made that clear."

"Maybe whoever it is decided you needed something a little more effective than a phone call."

"At least Phil Lester won't be waving a gun at me in noontime traffic anymore, will he?"

Nick didn't answer. She studied his face.

"You don't think it wasn't Lester on that bike today, do you?"

"My hunch is Lester was dead by that time."

A shiver went through her.

Nick stood. "You need some sleep."

"You're right." She rose, although she knew she would be awake for many hours. She had to brush by him in the narrow gap between the couch and the chair to get into the bedroom. That awkward moment came when they were chest to chest, the pose that preludes a kiss. He looked into her eyes, his expression never giving an inch but his voice tame when he said, "If you need anything, I'll be right here. Just yell."

He wasn't being suggestive. That scared her even more. Kindness could do things like that to her.

"Thanks, but I think I'm all set. I'll see you in the morning." She walked into the bedroom, leaving the door open as instructed, the light from the other room sufficient enough to see. The bed was unmade. This man needed a mother or a wife or a maid. She smoothed out the bottom sheet's wrinkles and crawled under the top sheet. She wiggled out of her shorts, dropped them on the floor. She unsnapped her bra, stretched her arms through the sleeves of her T-shirt to slide her bra off her arms. She lay in her ex-lover's bed in her shirt and underwear and a blanket of fear.

SHE WAS AWAKE when she heard him get up. The sounds in the kitchen signaled he was preparing coffee. It wasn't the first time he'd gotten up. Nor was it the first time she had awakened. He was a restless sleeper, getting up several times during the long night. She had seen him in the refrigerator's light. He would open and close the refrigerator door without removing anything. He'd cross to the window, the towers of the projects forming grids of light and dark across the glass. He'd move back to the recliner, click on the television, mute the sound, watch the silent pictures. He switched the channels frequently, old black-and-white movies, reruns of nineties sitcoms, infomercials. A visual lullaby until she herself had fallen into a fitful sleep, her dream images as hectic and disjointed as the changing pictures on the television screen. The next time she woke, the television was still on and Nick was stretched out in the recliner, but his snores joined the other night noises. She'd listened to the wheeze and wind of his breath telling her she wasn't alone.

She smelled coffee. Her eyes opened a slit. Nick passed the doorway in shorts and T-shirt and sneakers. The front door opened, closed. She groped for her shorts on the floor and wriggled into them under the sheet. By the time Nick returned from his run, his body sheened with sweat and smelling of hard exercise, she was on her third cup of black coffee.

He went to the fridge, pulled out a bottle of water, drank half of it before setting it on the counter. He wiped his mouth with the back of his bare arm. Cissy purposefully concentrated on stirring her coffee and feeling like a slug.

"Sorry if I woke you," he said.

"It wouldn't have taken much. How far do you run?"

"Until the demons stop chasing me." He didn't smile when he said it. Neither did she.

"How far today?"

He looked at her long and too intently for morning and only caffeine. "Not far enough," he said and walked to the bathroom.

She made the bed while he showered. She went into the living room, folded the sheet thrown in a heap on the couch, laid it on top the pillow and carried them into the bedroom, placed them at the foot of the bed. Her stomach rumbling, she went into the kitchen and opened the fridge, forced to test out her theory of personality on Nick. What she saw inside wasn't encouraging—beer, a take-out fast food bag, ketchup, its cap smeared red on the outside, a half-eaten jar of homemade marinated peppers someone must have given him and a pizza box that took up the whole second shelf. The water bottles, several of which were standing on a shelf on the inside of the door were the only thing that gave her hope.

"I would have shopped if I'd known I was having a guest," Nick said as he came into the kitchen, poured a cup of coffee.

She hadn't heard the shower stop. She shut the refrigerator. "You would have?" she said, always the skeptic.

He smiled. He had dressed for work. His hair was damp. His gun, cell phone, pager, handcuffs, badge waited on the table. "Nah."

She smiled back, grateful for his ability to make her smile at a time when it seemed a sacrilege.

"I'll buy you breakfast if you want to get dressed and go out."

She sat, unable not to look at the gun on the table. "I thought I was under house arrest."

"We've got two bodies now. No need to make it three."

Not your usual morning conversation. Then again, not your usual morning.

"I'm a big girl, Nick. I can handle myself."

He got up, dumped the rest of his cup of coffee

down the sink. He opened a drawer, put a key on the table. "Here's an extra key to the apartment."

"What about the rental car at Lester's?"

"I'll pick you up after work and take you to get it."

"And here I thought I was a free woman."

He strapped on his gun. He didn't smile. Neither did she. "You have my pager number? My cell?"

"And a key." She picked it up, waved it at him.

"Do me a favor."

She waited.

"Trust me."

She hadn't trusted anyone but herself since she was seventeen. Nick had been even younger. "You know better, Fiore."

He smiled. The attraction that was always there gained muscle.

"It was worth a shot." He gestured toward the bathroom. "There's towels and stuff. Help yourself."

"Thanks."

He walked to the fish tank, sprinkled some food into the tank, leaned down, tapped the glass. "Watch her, guys. She's a slippery one."

He straightened and faced her. "I gotta get to work." He didn't move, looked awkward for the first time Cissy could remember. She didn't know what was the matter, but she tried to help him out. "Have a good day," she said, Lucy to Ricky. Only after the words left her mouth did she realize how ludicrous they sounded.

"I've seen too many die, Cissy."

"And if it happens to me, you'll kill me?"

"Exactly." He moved toward the door, dropped a kiss on her crown as he passed, causing her to go very still. He was gone several minutes before she moved again. She got up, washed out her cup and the one Nick left in the sink, emptied the coffeepot, rinsed it and set it in the drainer. She walked around the apartment, went to the fish tank, tapped on the glass as Nick had done. Several pairs of protruding eyes blinked back at her.

"I know. He's right, isn't he, guys? I should lie low." That fact only made her more restless. She did some deep knee bends, jogged in place, trying to channel her nervous energy into something safe. She'd already seen one death. She didn't want to see another—especially her own. But at the same time, sitting around, waiting, seemed just as big a crime.

No reason she couldn't take a walk. A short one. She'd see if DiRisio's Bakery was still open, stop in for a pastry.

As she walked into the bedroom, she saw her purse on the floor, remembered the money. She couldn't be walking around with that kind of cash. She didn't know who it belonged to or why it was under her mother's front car seat, but she wanted it safe until she did. After going to the bakery, she'd find a bank nearby, rent a safety deposit box and put the money in there until she knew more about it.

She showered, was forced to dress in the same pair of shorts she'd worn yesterday, but took the tags off the other T-shirt she'd bought on sale, two for fifteen dollars. She considered skipping makeup. After yesterday, issues such as long, lustrous lashes suddenly seemed insane. But, as she'd learned last night, if anything was going to keep her from going over the edge, it was her little everyday routines. She wound her hair into a knot that stuck out every which way, a look waning in popularity now but not long ago was actually in vogue across the country. At least some reality could still make her smile. She borrowed a Yankees baseball cap for protection against the sun, threw it into her purse. She saw the fat blocks of cash. She stopped smiling.

The morning heat was young enough to feel only mildly oppressive. She started out at a brisk pace, arms swinging. *Until the demons are gone.*

She turned at the corner and cut through the park, quiet now except for the footfalls of joggers and the too easy, deep snores of the camped out homeless. She came out on the other side of the park and walked two blocks east to Central. At the next corner, she saw DiRisio's Bakery still thriving, the smell of their freshly baked pastries one of her sweeter childhood memories.

She went in to the tinkle of a bell above the door and the warmth of yeast and coffee. She circled round the bakery counter and the line of workers waiting for take-out to the main room with its curved counter and booths that looked out onto the avenue's traffic. Most of the customers were busy reading the daily edition. She sat down at the counter, ordered coffee and a nut horn in keeping with another of her life's philosophies that a person can never have too much black coffee and white sugar. She picked up a paper abandoned on the empty stool next to her and spread it on the counter.

Body Found On Barge was on the front page of the local section.

She looked up as her coffee and pastry came, hot and sweet as life should always be. "Thank you," she told the waitress. She took a bite and came back home to a memory of herself and her sister sent to get Sunday's rolls, sneaking one warm on the way home after finishing the Italian cookies Marie DiRisio always gave the children for free after telling them to be good girls. Her sister had been no more than six then, fresh-faced and fragile and full of life's possibilities. Cissy had been twelve. Jo Jo had idolized her. "Big sister" stuff. Cissy had left five years later. She swallowed hard, took a sip of coffee, didn't flinch when it burned her mouth. Jo Jo had picked the wrong hero that time, too. Cissy turned away from her memories to the paper.

Jacques Saint-Sault.

The body found on the ship last night had been identified. It was her sister's boyfriend.

Cissy read no further. Her mouth opened but she couldn't breathe. She leaned her chest against the counter, unable to look away from that name. She had known it could be him, but seeing it in black and white made it all too real. She bent closer to study the grainy picture of the port beside the article as if she looked hard enough, she would find them—her mother, her sister—peeking out from behind a corner, smiling, giving a little wave as if this were no more than the games of hide and seek she and Jo Jo used to play with the neighborhood children.

She dialed Nick.

"Fiore."

"It's him. Jo Jo's boyfriend. The guy. The body, the one they found." She was babbling. Not a good sign.

The waitress came to the counter. "Anything else, miss?"

"Where are you?" Nick demanded.

"I walked over to DiRisio's." She shook her head at the waitress. "I wanted a nut horn."

She listened to Nick's response. "Very colorful, officer."

The waitress tallied her bill, ripped it off her pad, laid it face-down on the counter and moved on.

"Did you get the robbery report Eddie filed on the gun?"

"Yeah."

"And?"

"You listen to me for the first time in your life, Spagnola. Your mother is missing. Your sister can't be found. Her boyfriend ends up junk in a trunk. Another body with a plug between the eyes ends up in your motel room—"

"Don't forget the attempt on my life yesterday."

The silence at the other end of the line told her she'd gone too far. "Don't you understand, Nick? If I hole up in your apartment, if I let them, whoever they may be, scare me, then I might as well put a bullet to my own brain right now, because they've already won. They'll have taken something from me, but I let them take it. And if I let them take it, I might never get it back.''

She heard a long breath on the other end of the line. ''Cut the crap, and get back to the apartment before you get your brains blown out.''

If it'd been a regular phone, Nick would have slammed it. Instead there was only a thin click. Cissy muttered a word that had once gotten her mouth washed out with soap by Sister Constance. She finished her coffee, forced herself to eat the pastry as one defiant act against death. She left a tip, walked to the register to pay.

''How was everything?''

Cissy didn't recognize the woman ringing her up behind the register. The DiRisios, like most Italian families, were large and varied. Many of the older ones brought their brothers, sisters, cousins over to live in the United States, help run the family business.

''Fine, fine,'' Cissy replied as if she hadn't just read her sister's boyfriend's body had been found stuffed in a trunk on a barge. The woman saw her glance at the platter of Italian cookies beside the register.

''For all our customers. Take some. Take some.'' The woman picked up two napkins from the pile beside the platter, set them in Cissy's palm, patted her hand. ''You enjoy them.''

''Thank you.'' Cissy looked at the platter of cookies, some pink, others dipped in thin chocolate, many covered with sprinkles that changed an ordinary day into a celebration. She chose two.

"Oh no, more, more. You too skinny." The old woman dropped four cookies onto the napkin, folded Cissy's fingers around them, gave her hand a final pat. "You come see us again. You good girl, I can tell."

Cissy turned away. Six and twelve they'd been, her and her sister. It could have been yesterday.

She walked toward the door. *I won't leave you this time,* she promised her sister, her mother. *I won't let you down again.*

Chapter Eight

Nick set the photo on the bar. The bartender angled his gaze, whistled through his teeth.

"Know him?"

The bartender leaned over the counter, licked his lips.

"That the man Jo Jo Spagnola used to meet here?"

"Looks like him, except for the hair. This guy's bald as a hard-boiled egg."

"He must have worn a piece."

The bartender turned and poured a glass of gin, offered it to Nick, who shook his head. The bartender toasted to both their health, then drained the glass and dropped it in the sink. "That'd explain the good hair."

Nick took the picture. "Anyone else been in to see you, asking questions about Jo Jo Spagnola?"

"Should I be expecting someone?"

"A woman might come in here, wanting to talk to you. Blond, beautiful."

The bartender lifted a brow, his expression one of amusement.

Gin on an empty stomach, Nick figured. "Big sister."

"Blond, beautiful, big sister." The bartender hissed.

Nick smiled with surprising ease, a mirthless smile. "She asks, you answer. Little as possible. Don't get chummy."

The bartender straightened an arm garter. "Do I look the chummy type?"

Nick walked calmly toward the exit. "The jury's still out on that, sweet pea."

CISSY WAS OPENING the door when she heard someone call her name. She turned and saw Tommy Marcus next to the glass bakery case.

"Let me pay, and I'll be right with you." He handed money to the cashier and came toward Cissy.

"What brings you out so bright and early?" He juggled his coffee and bag so he could open the door for her.

"A craving."

"God bless them. Come, walk with me to my car."

Outside the door, he slowed his pace. "Cissy, tell me if I'm getting too personal here—" He paused, Cissy sensed, as much for drama as to gauge her reaction. He would make a fine politician one day. "I hear you come home, and it's not good. The family."

She tasted the pastry, too sugary inside her mouth. "Too bad you don't hear anything I don't know."

"Hey." He held up his palms. "I don't mean to insult."

Neither had she. It was that boyish face—a combination of Beaver Cleaver and young Danny Kaye in *Boystown*—that put her on edge, made her fear she would pour out her guts to him as if he were a padre.

"I don't mean to insult either, Tommy. It's my—" The words stayed in her throat like the pastry's sweetness. She didn't want to say them one more time.

He nodded. "I hear about your mother, your sister." He crossed himself.

Lapsed Catholic or not, she joined him and said a quick prayer.

"Last night they found a body on a ship docked in the port. This morning I read it's a guy Jo Jo's hung with. She's missing and he shows up stuffed in a ceiling tile." The frustration swelled inside her, dangerously close to spilling over in some destructive or embarrassing way. She held on tighter to her purse strap.

Tommy laid a hand on her forearm. "I know some people—"

It was the neighborhood motto.

"In the precinct. Maybe I make sure your mother and sister's case gets top priority?"

"I appreciate the offer." *Don't take no favors, Cissy.* Her motto. "But Nick's on the case."

"He's a good cop."

She nodded.

"Who would have thought it, huh?"

She smiled.

"Any leads on your mother and sister?"

"My stepfather, Eddie, says he came home from

work and my mother was gone. Nothing left but her car and some dry cleaning tickets. He says she ran out on him.''

''You believe him?''

She looked straight at Tommy. ''I wish to God it were the truth.''

He didn't fill in with the obligatory ''Everything will be okay.'' He, too, had grown up on the lower side.

''What about your sister?''

Cissy shrugged. ''Jo Jo has been known to get lost for days, weeks on end....'' She didn't need to fill in the blanks for Tommy.

''There's a program, you know, over off of Green. Assemblyman Brunelli got the funding doubled for it in last year's budget. They don't do magic but they have had some success.''

''Jo Jo's been through a couple of programs.''

''No luck?'' She heard the sympathy in his voice.

''They don't do magic.'' Her voice was not unkind. Her smile was sad. ''Mama prays. Last time I talked to her, she said Jo Jo was doing better.'' Her voice caught. She grew angry with herself. ''Mama always had too much hope in people.''

''It's hard on mothers.''

''Yeah.'' Cissy looked the length of the street.

''It's hard on everybody.''

She shrugged. It didn't do any good to get sentimental on the streets.

''Cissy, you need anything, you call me.''

''Thanks, Tommy. I appreciate it.''

"Hey, what are old friends for? Where you staying?"

"Nick's."

He'd learned enough from dealing with politicians not to strike a sidelong glance.

"He thinks it's the safest place for me."

"What do you think?" Tommy of the streets smiled, not needing airs with her after all.

An image of Nick in no more than shorts and a smile came into her mind. She thought she was doomed. "What are old friends for?"

He smiled, draped his arm around her shoulders. "Under different circumstances, I'd have asked you out to dinner by now."

With the Beaver Cleaver-Boystown gig going for him, Cissy had never thought of Tommy in that light. Even though her mother had done her damnedest.

"Maybe when everything settles down. Next week or the next, if you're still around."

The simple phrase, "if you're still around," sent a chill through her. "I appreciate the invite, but I'm not very good company lately."

"Give me more time to brag about my accomplishments."

She smiled. He was a sweet man. Successful, too. Just her luck she always went for sex appeal over sensible and safe. She could hear the general chorus of mothers in the neighborhood, throughout the land: "But he's such a good boy."

She looked at Tommy, thought of Nick. There'd never be any fireworks but that only meant less chance of getting burnt. "You know what, I'd like to have dinner with you, once I'm not so preoccupied with everything." Contrary to her earlier fears, she had gotten a little wiser in the last fifteen years.

Tommy smiled. "Here's my car." They'd stopped before a white Lincoln. "Can I drop you anywhere?"

Cissy shook her head.

He handed her his card. "You need anything, anything at all, you call my office. Day or night. If I'm not there, the service will take a message, get it to me."

"Thanks, Tommy."

He leaned over, pecked her cheek. "You promise?"

Such a good boy.

"I promise."

After he drove off, she walked three blocks to a branch of the First Trust. All the safety deposit boxes were rented at this location but some were available at their central headquarters downtown. Cissy caught the bus. It wasn't even ten-thirty, but already the humidity had thickened like Mama Napoli's sauce. On the way, the bus passed the Golden Cue. Cissy made a note of its location. A few blocks farther, Cissy waved to Gentleman George on the corner, looking uncommonly jaunty even in this heat. She got off several stops later and rented a box at the bank. Taking advantage of the small private room, she examined the cash. All twenties. A quick assessment revealed there was more than she'd thought. Easily fifty thousand. Maybe a hundred thousand. The amount worried her. Where would her mother get that kind of cash? If it even belonged to her. Had someone stashed it there, trying to frame her mother? Eddie? Jo Jo had used the car, too. Was it hers? Why didn't she take it with her? She stared at the money as if the answers could be found in two stacks of twenties.

She left the bank, her handbag lighter. She called Al's Auto Palace. The Thunderbird wouldn't be ready until tomorrow at the earliest. She dialed Nick as she started back uptown.

"Where are you?" was his hello.

"Heading uptown. Any news on my mother and sister?" she interjected before Nick could start harassing her to go back to the apartment.

"I'm working a few leads."

"Such as?"

She passed an office building, the travel agency on its ground floor with a poster of palm trees and white beaches and people with perfect bodies in scanty bathing suits spread cruelly across its storefront window.

"So you're on your way back to the apartment?" Nick ignored her question.

Suddenly, in the storefront's reflection, she thought she saw a man across the street, watching her. She moved slowly to the next storefront.

"Cissy? Are you there?"

She feigned interest in the shoes displayed in the store's window. The man was medium height, wore his dark hair in a crew cut and was still watching her.

The Harlequin Reader Service® — Here's how it works:

ccepting your 2 free books and mystery gift places you under no obligation to buy anything. You may keep the books and gift and return e shipping statement marked "cancel." If you do not cancel, about a month later we'll send you 6 additional books and bill you just 1.99 each in the U.S., or $4.74 each in Canada, plus 25¢ shipping & handling per book and applicable taxes if any.* That's the complete ce and — compared to cover prices of $4.75 each in the U.S. and $5.75 each in Canada — it's quite a bargain! You may cancel at any ne, but if you choose to continue, every month we'll send you 6 more books, which you may either purchase at the discount price or urn to us and cancel your subscription.

erms and prices subject to change without notice. Sales tax applicable in N.Y. Canadian residents will be charged applicable provincial es and GST. Credit or debit balances in a customer's account(s) may be offset by any other outstanding balance owed by or to the stomer.

NO POSTAGE
NECESSARY
IF MAILED
IN THE
UNITED STATES

BUSINESS REPLY MAIL
FIRST-CLASS MAIL   PERMIT NO. 717-003   BUFFALO, NY

POSTAGE WILL BE PAID BY ADDRESSEE

HARLEQUIN READER SERVICE
3010 WALDEN AVE
PO BOX 1867
BUFFALO NY 14240-9952

Play the Lucky Hearts Game

and get...

2 FREE BOOKS

and a **FREE MYSTERY GIFT...**

Yes! YOURS to KEEP!

I have scratched off the silver card. Please send me my *2 FREE BOOKS* and *FREE mystery GIFT*. I understand that I am under no obligation to purchase any books as explained on the back of this card.

Scratch Here!

then look below to see what your cards get you... 2 Free Books & a Free Mystery Gift!

382 HDL DU6Z   **182 HDL DU7H**

FIRST NAME   LAST NAME

ADDRESS

APT.#   CITY

STATE/PROV.   ZIP/POSTAL CODE   (H-I-08/03)

Twenty-one gets you **2 FREE BOOKS** and a **FREE MYSTERY GIFT!**

Twenty gets you **2 FREE BOOKS!**

Nineteen gets you **1 FREE BOOK!**

TRY AGAIN!

Offer limited to one per household and not valid to current Harlequin Intrigue® subscribers. All orders subject to approval.

"Yes. Nick, I think someone is watching me. A man across the street."

"What's he look like?"

"He's—" She hesitated as the man disappeared into an office building. "Never mind," she said. "He just walked into an office building." Feeling foolish, she moved away from the store window. "Obviously my imagination is working overtime." Embarrassed, she changed the subject. "Ran into Tommy Marcus at breakfast. He told me to call him if I needed anything."

"Yeah, and what do you need?"

"For starters, a car. My mother's car won't be ready until tomorrow at the earliest." Several blocks up, she spied the neon sign of the Golden Cue rendered neutral by the bright sun. "I want to pick up the rental."

"We'll get it tonight. I'll pick you up after my shift. So, you're on your way home now?"

Home. She turned a corner, closing in on the Golden Cue.

"Cissy, you're on your way home." It wasn't a question this time.

A customer went inside the Golden Cue's doors. The bar was open.

"I just have one or two stops to make on the way. I'll see you tonight." She clicked off before Nick could protest and headed toward the Golden Cue.

Before television, video games and singles bars, every city worth its salt had at least one pool hall, usually more. But in recent years, many halls had closed, been converted or torn down completely to make room for warehouse stores or fitness centers. On entering, Cissy could tell the Golden Cue had attempted to avoid its fate by going respectable in an effort to attract an upscale crowd who called pool billiards and could be hustled by Cissy's second-grade teacher, Sister Agatha, should she ever have the inclination. New lights had been strung over each table. A sign above the bar advertised Cosmopolitans and a complete wine list. The bartender was handsome in a fey way, not helped by the black arm garters on his sleeves and the pelvis grin of his too-tight pants. Not that Cissy was one to judge, but anyone from the neighborhood with any standards left wouldn't be caught dead in here. Lucky for the bartender, who would have gotten beaten up on a weekly basis by the hall's original crowd. Still, despite the accoutrements of a respectable sport, the place smelled of smoke and the swift con. Besides that, what had Jo Jo been doing hanging out here?

Cissy sauntered over to the bar. She didn't know her sister to shoot pool much, but she did know her to drink. If anyone was fast friends with Jo Jo, it was the bartender.

He came toward her with a satisfied smile and an offer to serve. At least this was one place she could order a spring water with lemon and not get blacklisted. Some small groups were clustered by the tables but there were no other customers at the bar. The bartender set her drink on an eight-ball coaster.

"Player?" He indicated the tables with a tip of his head.

"No, not me. Have some friends that like the game, though. Maybe you know one of them?"

"Maybe." The bartender hedged his bets.

"Jo Jo Spagnola."

The bartender showed no recognition. Cissy's heart sank.

"Small girl in her mid-twenties. Pretty." Jo Jo was young enough the drugs hadn't ravaged her looks yet. By thirty-five, she would look sixty.

"Long, thick black hair, dark brown eyes, likes to snap her gum to music." She hadn't even realized she'd remembered that habit.

The bartender's face gave away nothing.

"She might have come in here with a guy." She didn't say a name. If the bartender read the papers, watched the news, he might become leery.

The bartender leaned against the glossy bar. "Who's asking?"

He did know Jo Jo. Cissy kept her expression neutral. "Her sister."

He smiled. "Big sister?"

"What else?" Cissy wiped her hand damp from being wrapped around the glass on her shorts and extended it. "Cissy Spagnola."

"Otto Chandler." The bartender shook her hand in one of those boneless shakes designed to make either her or him feel like a lady.

The bartender blew out a breath. "Jo Jo's sister, huh?"

"You know her?"

"You the hotshot stockbroker?"

That was her current story and she was sticking to it. "She mention me?"

"Tell you the truth, I thought she made you up."

"I don't get home much." *Home.* Damn, she refused to feel guilty or crazy.

"And when you do, I bet you don't hang out in pool halls."

"I thought it was called billiards nowadays."

They shared a grin.

"So, Jo Jo's meeting you here?"

"Actually I was hoping you might have seen her. I just got into town yesterday. Thought I'd surprise her but the number I have is disconnected. I wasn't sure of the address."

The bartender assessed her with a steady gaze. Despite the uptown appearance, he was no whipping boy. Cissy would've laid down money he wasn't as fond of those arm garters as he appeared to be.

"Place where she last worked told me sometimes she would hang here."

"She's been in here."

"Care to elaborate?"

"Maybe."

Gone was the good-time guy.

"Maybe I should tell the liquor board there's people under twenty-one without an adult in a place that serves liquor in the middle of the day." She surprised herself.

"So what? I ain't serving them."

Oops. Gone was the slick style now, a reversion to his roots. She had him on the ropes.

"How 'bout I take a smell of their drinks?

Otto leaned his face to hers. "Go ahead."

He called her bluff. She had nothing else and he could smell it. She reached into her purse and pulled out a couple of the loose twenties she'd found stuffed in Cherry's seat cushions, making a mental IOU to her mother. Otto looked at the bills, unimpressed.

"C'mon, Jo Jo's not on the Ten Most Wanted."

"Are you sure?"

"Very funny." She tapped the twenties. "Go on, take it, get yourself some new arm garters."

"I'll bet that smart mouth has gotten you into a lot of trouble."

"I bet those garters have gotten you in a lot of trouble."

His gaze stayed heavy on her, but he slowly picked up the twenties and folded them into his wallet.

"Your sister used to come in, hang out at the bar until her friend came."

"Who was her friend?"

The bartender straightened, shrugged one shoulder. "Like some of the after-five crowd that comes in here. Businessman. Had an intellectual look about him. Studied the table as if determining the trajectory projection of each shot. Couldn't shoot worth a crap."

Cissy smiled. "You got a name?"

Otto shook his head.

"No name?"

"He never came up to the bar. Stayed in the back.

Your sister would get the drinks. Paid the tab in cash. Always left a good tip.''

"How often did she meet him here?"

"When I was on, about twice a week. More often the last month.''

Two customers had come in. The bartender left to serve them, signaling her money was up. She pulled another twenty out of her purse. She reached for her water and took a long swallow, turning in her stool to give the place a final once-over. The bartender came back, eyed the twenty.

She set her glass down on it. "Anything else you can tell me about the guy my sister was meeting?"

He looked at the twenty. She lifted her glass. It had sweated a wet ring on the bill. She slid the money toward him.

"What'd he look like?"

"Like I told you, a regular-looking businessman.''

"Tall? Short?"

"Medium.''

Cissy sighed. "How about his hair? Long? Short? Blond? Brown? Black?"

"Dark, brown, thick.'' He smiled. "Kennedy hair.'' His hand fisted over the twenty. He pulled out his wallet, slid the cash inside, indicating again her time was up.

"That's it? Nothing else?" She scribbled her phone number on the coaster, pushed it toward him.

He glanced down, but didn't pick up the coaster. He lifted his gaze. "Ask Detective Fiore.''

She went out into a sun strong enough to turn ta

to putty and normal thoughts murderous. She pulled out her phone, left a message on Nick's voice mail to call her. She passed the bus stop at the corner, but decided to walk her fury off for a few minutes.

Her shirt was stuck to her back by the time she hit the crosswalk. Her anger showed no sign of cooling, either. Nick might think he had her best interests at heart, but the man was going to send her over the edge more quickly than the ninety-one percent humidity. She bought a soda from a sidewalk vendor, drank it as the crosstown bus pulled up at the next stop. She had almost made it when the bus's doors began to close. She gave a banshee yell that felt damn good and the doors opened. She jumped on and sat down, panting, as she headed to the river and Eddie's bar. When she got off at the stop near the bar, she saw Eddie's burgundy Mercury in the side alley. She'd started toward the tavern when a dark sedan pulled up in front of the building. She ducked into the nearest open doorway. Through the name etched on the door, Body Designs by Dimitri, she watched Nick get out of the car, go into Fat Eddie's.

"Yes-s-s-s?" she heard on a long exhale behind her. She turned to a man smoking a slim cigar. She assumed he was Dimitri, if there even was a Dimitri.

Inhaling, he considered her. He was slender with a blue silk scarf around his neck and a sashay to his walk that made Cissy admire him immediately. Any man who wore silk scarves and sashayed in the south side and had lived to tell about it had her respect.

"You wish some body art, perhaps?"

Cissy looked around. Actually she had had moments when she'd considered indulging in the current tattoo trend. Just a small one around her ankle, or maybe along the curve of her lower back to add some interest when she went to the beach.

"You hesitate. You are afraid, perhaps?"

"I'm not afraid."

Dimitri adopted a skeptical smile. She wasn't fooling anyone anymore.

She looked back to the street. She wouldn't be able to talk to Eddie until Nick left. The view from Dimitri's window was perfect. From this angle, she could even see the side of the bar and enough of the back if anyone went in or out through that entrance. Besides, she reasoned as she turned toward Dimitri and his cheeky smile, who knew how many bikini days she had left?

Chapter Nine

Eddie was at a table on the phone when Nick walked into the bar. He hung up as Nick came toward the table. He didn't get up. He didn't invite Nick to sit.

"Little Nicky Fiore. How's the family?"

"That's funny. I was just about to ask you the same thing, Eddie."

He picked up a cigar butt from an ashtray, chewed on it. "That is funny."

"Heard from Louisa or Jo Jo?"

He looked at Nick, his eyes full of nothing. "They ain't sent no postcards."

"You seem real broken up."

He leaned forward, killed the cigar. "The broad left me. I'm crushed."

"Left her car, too."

"Probably doesn't want me to find her."

"Why's that?"

"Because I'd kill her." He relaxed back, his tiny eyes half-closed.

"Heard you let Jo Jo take the car that night?"

"I'm a nice guy like that. How's my other stepdaughter, the smart-ass one? Heard she's keeping you hopping.''

"You watching her?''

"I'm a family man—what can I say?'' Eddie's lips curled into a fat sneer.

Nick leaned on the table with a leaden stare. "Me, too, Eddie. Sixteen years is too long to wait.''

Nick saw Eddie's hand twitch atop the table.

"I've been patient. And I'm not a patient man.''

Eddie reached for a new cigar, stuck it between his lips. A still, fixed look came into his eyes. "I got things to do, Fiore.'' His smile stayed mean.

Nick straightened, kept the threat thick in his voice. "Me, too, Eddie.''

FROM THE TATTOO parlor's window, Cissy saw Nick leave the bar. She waited until his dark sedan disappeared down the street.

"Gotta go, Dimitri.'' She started to get up.

"Whoa, wait, crazy lady. I have to wipe with antiseptic, put a bandage on.''

She sighed, sat down. Hard to argue with a guy who wore blue silk in the port. She propped up her leg. In the end, she'd chosen a small abstract design on her ankle instead of her lower back. She'd decided that twenty years from now, when her butt was heading toward her knees, she'd regret calling attention to that part of her body.

"Leave this on overnight.'' Dimitri applied a small bandage. She pulled out cash as he recited other care instructions, paid him and hurried to the door.

She was about to step outside when she saw Eddie round the corner from the back of the bar and head toward the street. She stepped back from sight, watched until he'd walked to the next block before she opened the door and followed him. She caught sight of him as he turned the corner. She hurried until she saw him again. She slowed, careful to lag several feet behind the cover of other pedestrians. He headed toward the river walk that stretched from the business district to the lower end. He turned once. She stopped, pretending interest in an appliance-shop window. She threw a sidelong look in Eddie's direction. He was continuing toward the river walk.

She followed him to the riverfront. Several years ago tax dollars had built the walkway that also boasted a bike path, benches and food vendors.

Eddie walked a quarter mile before sitting down on a bench. He took a wad of tissues out of his pocket and wiped his face.

Cissy watched from the street, blocked by a Mr. Ding-A-Ling ice cream truck. Eddie sat. He pulled the hem of his short-sleeved shirt from his pants waistband and reached beneath the shirt. Cissy went on full alert, but all he pulled out was a wide support belt that must have been wrapped around his bulging waistline to support the lower back muscles. He laid it on the bench beside him. Eddie and exercise? Cissy wasn't buying it.

He sat like that for several more minutes. Bike riders passed, in-line skaters, a woman pushing a double stroller with one child struggling to get out of the back seat, a nun in a navy blue habit who elicited Cissy's sympathy. Not that she thought nuns sweated. Cissy bought an ice pop from Mr. Ding-A-Ling. From that distance, she couldn't see any expression on Eddie's face. After about twenty minutes, he stood and headed back to the bar. Staying out of sight, she followed. A block behind him, she saw him get into his Mercury. She ducked into the shadows of a doorway as the car passed, and she stood there chewing on a Popsicle stick, the heat and her frustration at the same dangerous level.

With nothing more to show than a tattoo and the knowledge she was never going to get any information with Nick one step ahead of her, she decided to head back to the apartment and talk her next move over with the fish. As she stepped out of the doorway, she saw a man in a baseball cap and shorts a half block away. He looked familiar. She was becoming as paranoid as a politician.

She caught the bus and got out at a corner store several stops before Nick's building. She bought cheese, crackers, a liter of soda, and a six-pack of imported beer for Nick. She was angry, but also a good guest. As she waited to pay for her purchases, she glanced out the store window, spying the same man in shorts and baseball cap she'd seen near Fat Eddie's. Coincidence, she tried to convince herself. The man took off the cap to wipe his brow. He had a black crew cut. She recognized the man she'd seen downtown earlier.

She left the store, headed toward Nick's with a

nonchalance she'd never had the privilege of feeling in her life. The street was busy, the sidewalk crowded with students, shoppers, workers ducking out for a quick break. Cissy weaved in and around the others, away from her unknown fan. She glanced back. The man was strolling up the street with the same checked calm as she. She crossed at the corner, still several long blocks from Nick's building. She quickened her steps, the sweat slick along her shoulders, trickling down her spine.

The streets farther from central downtown were less populated. She dared to throw another look over her shoulder. A quick scan didn't reveal the man. Had she been imagining it? Still, she quickened her steps and turned at the next corner. The street headed into the park, almost empty due to the strong sun and unbearable heat. Thick stands of trees and high bushes edged the park's path, providing shade but also secret cover where deeds not fit for human eyes could be done undetected.

Cutting through the park was the shortest way to Nick's apartment, but that meant taking the path that provided opportunities for...she didn't even want to think what opportunities abounded in the park's recesses. She had to go one block back if she chose the longer route, risking the chance of running smack into her stalker. She shot a glance over her shoulder, saw nothing. She was still moving toward the park, unsure what she was going to do, when she spied an alley between two tall buildings. She ducked inside, greeted by the odor of human waste and broken wine bottles. Until she passed the Dumpster she didn't see a steel storage building at the other end of the alley, its door locked and bolted. A half-ton pickup parked perpendicular to the alley blocked exit from that end. She turned back to the street, peeked her head out, snapped it back as the man with the baseball cap came around the corner.

She hid behind the far side of the Dumpster, the bag of groceries and six-pack of beer beside her. Nauseous from fear and the smells heated by the sun, she waited.

Through a crack between the Dumpster and the wall she saw a shadow stretch across the sidewalk in front of the alley's opening. She held her breath, her clammy back flattened to the brick wall, stray hairs pasted to her neck. The man in the baseball cap paused. Her flesh prickled as he peered into the alley. She waited. Nothing. She peeked between the Dumpster and the wall, saw only the sun's blinding reflection across the sidewalk. She released a breath and stood. She was bending to pick up the groceries when her cell phone rang.

She froze. The phone rang again. She sank back behind the Dumpster, fumbled for the slim receiver. The man was too far away to hear the phone, she told herself. One eye trained to the slit between the Dumpster and the wall, she clutched the phone and whispered, "Hello?"

"Cissy?"

Nick. Relief so rich, she forgave him everything, past, present and future.

A figure moved into the alleyway's entrance. Nick called her name as the phone fell from her hand into her purse. Her fingers severed the connection, turned off the ringer.

The man moved cautiously into the alley. She had thought herself safe. How many times had she made the same mistake?

Keeping her gaze on the approaching figure, she reached toward the six-pack, wrapped one hand around a bottle's long neck, her other hand around another. She brought both hands together, hoisted the bottles to her shoulder, preparing to strike.

The man's shadow started past the end of the Dumpster. She stood and swung as hard as she could into the man's groin. Bull's-eye. With a groan, the man went down and hit with a thud so hard, even Cissy jumped.

He lay facedown in the dirt, moaning. The back of his T-shirt pulled tight outlined the holstered gun and the police badge clipped to the man's belt.

CISSY PACED the apartment beneath the fish's placid regard.

"It's not enough telling every possible lead not to talk to me? You had the police follow me?"

Nick poured one of the beers from the six-pack that had taken his colleague down. He took a sip, his cool rivaling his pets'. "It was for your protection."

"I don't need protection."

He took another sip as if considering her statement. "Spinelli would probably agree with you there."

Cissy winced. "I am sorry about that."

Nick waved away her worry. "The ribbing he takes from the department will be more painful." He gave a short laugh. "Taken out by a six-pack."

"If you hadn't had him following me, none of this would have happened."

He stood and set the beer bottle on the counter. "Spinelli's a rookie hot to play detective. The chief thought it was a good way to keep him busy and keep an eye on you."

"I'm a suspect?"

"You broke in to Lester's house the night he was found murdered. Later he was found in your motel room."

She stared at him. "Is that what you think? That I murdered Lester, then plopped him in my room to take the suspicion off me?"

"No, that's not what I think. But the rest of the department doesn't know you like I do."

She thought he was playing with her until he didn't smile.

"They don't know that you let Mary Elizabeth Goca pierce your ears with an ice cube and sewing needle when you were eleven and your mother grounded you for a month. Or that you thought your feet were too big when you were thirteen and nearly crippled yourself wearing shoes three sizes too small to stop your feet from growing. Or that at fourteen, you let your little sister fall asleep with her head in your lap on our couch while my mother took yours to General for X rays."

He stepped toward her.

"They don't know you feel as helpless and afraid as you did twenty years ago."

But he did. Because he'd been right there. Because he'd experienced the same anger and frustration and fear.

Her gaze dropped away from his sinfully handsome face, only to be stopped by the hard length of his body, the lean legs, the abdomen that rippled beneath the shirt tight to his wide shoulders. She raised her gaze to find him assessing her with the same hypnotic interest. His lids, thick lashed, lowered, his face increasing its sensual cast. Her breath hitched. She had to save her mother and sister. But she had no idea who was going to save her.

He stepped closer in a movement that was as much to seduce as it was to dominate. She wouldn't have stepped away if her feet had been on fire. "You were lucky today."

"Was I?" She was pleased by the layer of huskiness infusing her voice, causing the heavy-lidded lust in her ex-lover's eyes to thicken.

He blinked. The sensuality became seriousness. "Whatever your mother and sister got mixed up in, these guys aren't playing around. This isn't cops and robbers to them. It's life and death. *Your* death if you're in the way."

He'd come too near, but there was no threat or power play or even breath-stealing lust. What was left was something wonderful. A solid man. She wanted to put her arms around him and let him pull her close.

Let the weight of her body relent, if only for an il-
lusionary moment. Her need made her angry. When
she looked up into his dark eyes and had to plead,
she became angrier still. "Are they alive, Nick?"

He pulled her into his arms, tight to his body. Her
hands balled up into ineffective fists and pressed
against his chest. "I'll find them, Cissy."

This was Nick. She didn't know how many morals
he'd lost or gained in the fifteen years since she'd last
been in his arms, but she did know he didn't make
promises he couldn't keep.

She rested her forehead against his chest, too tired
to pretend to pull away. Holding her shoulders strong
so they wouldn't shake, she allowed two tears to slip
down her cheeks. Just as quickly she stopped them.
She'd be damned if they'd make her cry. She'd let
them shoot her first.

She lifted her head, Nick's lips so close she died
to touch them, take their warmth and comfort so
openly offered. Warmth that rallied against murder
and death. She had to taste life. The warmth that ex-
ploded into heat as she flicked her tongue across the
softness of his bottom lip. With a groan he sealed her
lips with his own and plunged inside her, hot and
thick and dizzying as the day's heat. Her body swayed
to his, the arousal of her nipples rubbing against the
broad span of his chest, the pressure of her pelvis
meeting his in open arousal. He kissed her harder,
pulling away to plant a trail of kisses down her throat,
find the curve of her ear and trace it with his tongue.
She dipped her head, taking his mouth hard and fully,

desire and the thought of death demanding nothing else but these lips, this body, this man. Her hands crept up the wonderful slopes and shifts of his back. She cupped his face with her hands, her palms to his cheeks and the new sweetness of his lips even scarier than the heavy, pulsing lust.

Nick pulled away, muttered thickly, "Damn," his breathing ragged. His gaze came back to her, black and serious.

"I can promise you I'll find out what happened to your mother and sister. I won't promise anything else."

Nick Fiore with a conscience. He'd make her love him yet. Her pelvis was still joined with the hardness of his own arousal, her legs still trembling from his touch and his taste. She pressed her body to him harder. "Hell of a time to get serious, Fiore."

But as he laughed, dropping his mouth to cover hers once more with a passion all the more appealing in its forced restraint, she knew he was right. From the moment she'd looked up in the station house, the sight of him slamming into her with breath-stealing, body-rocking force, she'd known. She'd lost. The fight was over before it'd even begun.

She pulled away, already regretting the space between their bodies. But they weren't teens anymore, when passion was pure and simple and without thought. They were complex, responsible adults. Sex was infinitely possible and even more pleasurable than in their heady youth, but life was more than random orgasms. She faced Nick, with his face made for dreams and his body made for desire, his sexuality raw as the regret that ripped through her. He waited, his thoughts always without revelation, his invulnerable expression no help at all. She reached for him, releasing a word that would have resulted in three Hail Marys and three Our Fathers at Saturday confessional. She had lost a long time ago. Like her mother and sister now, she'd been among the missing ever since.

His body hardened at the feel of her. The rush of desire staggered her.

He looked down at her, a concern in his dark eyes that she knew surprised him as much as her.

"You should stay away from me."

She went on tiptoe and pressed her mouth to his. "I can't do that, Fiore." In for a penny, in for a pound.

His hands tightened on her shoulders. She thought for a second he was going to shake her as if she'd lost her mind. Then with a low growl he pulled her against him, their bodies meeting with the boldness that had always been between them. One hand tangled possessively in her hair, forcing her head back, angling it for pleasure. With a harsh intake of breath, his mouth came crushing down on hers. He thrust into her, delving deep into the warmth of her mouth. Her mouth curved in a smile. She would have laughed aloud with a wanton fever if not for the complete capture of her mouth beneath his. His hand tightened on the back of her head possessively, controlling her, pressing her harder still to him. But it was his other hand fisted in the back of her shirt, pressed to her backbone, that gave him away.

She stopped, drew back from him, the quiver in her knees causing her body to weave. He wrapped his arms around her to steady her. She looked into his eyes for a long moment. If the bad guys didn't kill her, Nick Fiore would.

Chapter Ten

She slid her hands up the nape of his neck and pulled his head down, brushing her lips against his tenderly, tantalizingly as her body melded to his, her pelvis following the rhythm of her lips. Her tongue slid inside his mouth, caressing his teeth, the roof of his mouth. She touched her tongue to his, stroked it, played with it until they both groaned and their breath moved harsh and shuddering and even her reeling Catholic conscience fell away, leaving her shameless and wanting him, fiercely, hungrily, more than she had ever wanted anything in her whole life.

Her lips inches from him, she whispered, ''Been getting awful brave lately, haven't I?'' She wanted him to know she was scared. Scared as he.

He tipped her chin. ''Tough girl.'' His eyes remained fixed on her. He was waiting for her. He never rushed. He didn't have to.

She stroked the nape of his neck. She would be sorry, but it would be the sweetest regret she'd ever had. She opened her mouth and surrendered her soul.

''Make love to me, Nick.''

He took her mouth in a kiss so slow and devouring, if she hadn't fallen in love with him before, she would have now. As it was, she only admitted to herself in lustful delirium what she'd always feared. She'd prayed it'd been a fluke or the embellishment of memory that happens easily over time. But fifteen years later, no man had made her feel the same as when she'd opened her legs—and her heart—to Nick Fiore.

The sweet torment grew urgent. Her mouth opened, matching his passion, while her hands tugged his shirt from the waistband of his pants, slid beneath the fabric to the smooth span of his back, caressing his strong shoulders, cool skin.

His mouth crushed hers greedily. His fingers gathered the fabric of her shirt, drew it over her head. His hand, heated, strong, cupped her breast, released it from the confines of her bra to close over it. His touch delighted in her breasts' silken full curves, her nipples puckered with desire. The pad of his index finger stroked, circled the nipple's tip, causing Cissy to shiver with pleasure. His mouth trailed down her throat, the fine flesh of her upper chest, closing over her bare breast, caressing it with the hot, moist heat of his mouth. Clutching his shoulders, her back arched and her fingernails drew blood.

Her arms wrapped around him and she clung to him as he released her only to cup her breasts with both hands, stroking, molding while his mouth and tongue caressed and her body writhed against him, her moans of pleasure long and shuddering.

He lifted her in his arms, carried her to his bed, where he'd once promised her she'd be safe. She looked up to find his mouth hard and taut and his black eyes fierce with desire. Cradled against his hard chest, he kissed her long and slow and deep before gently lowering her to the bed as if to say, "You're still safe." They both knew they weren't.

He laid her on the bed she'd made that morning and found her mouth, hungry and hot and urgent. She unbuttoned his shirt and pushed it off his shoulders. She marveled at his beauty, her fingers tracing a rippled abdomen like a blind person reading Braille. With a pleased laugh, he smoothed the hair back from her face, quickly kissed her mouth, moved down her body, kissing the shape of her until the hot, heavy throbbing between her legs pleaded for release. She reached for him, wanting him, wanting to pleasure him and telling him in language breathless and base and pleasing to both their ears. With a wildfire in his eyes, he took her gaze, held it as he unsnapped her shorts, yanked them to her knees, leaned down to open his mouth against the panties covering the apex of her legs. The damp heat of his mouth burned through the thin silk. He pressed hips, lips and tongue and teeth against her, nibbling, biting, licking while her blood pounded in her head, between her legs and in the most unresponsive of muscles, her heart.

He slid the panties down to her knees only to return to her, exposed and anxious for him, his tongue finding her sweet spot, caressing it hot and wet with a slow slither that made her cry out, ache to part her thighs and give him greater access but finding herself bound at the knees and helpless beneath the weight of him and the touch of him. Her hips undulated, her body writhed, needful, hungry, while each leisurely stroke brought her closer to ecstasy.

He took her wrists, pinned them at her sides as his tongue and mouth took her higher in sweet, sexual torture until she arched, pressing herself deeper against his mouth. She climaxed with a shuddering cry ripped from inside her and filled with joyous release.

She did not open her eyes for a long time afterward, still somewhere between heaven and earth and not anxious to leave. When she did open them, her lids heavy, her limbs languid, she found Nick watching her. His eyes glittering, he smiled a slow smile that acknowledged her passion, relished it and promised more.

He stripped them both, Cissy watching with the pleased afterglow of passion, enjoying the naked sight of him. She reached for him. He came down on top of her, his weight and strength a wonderful thing in a world where so little was solid. She explored, knowing his urgency, surprised to find her own building again with lazy licks of fire promising to burst into flame.

He parted her legs with his thigh, kissed her until the flames grew again, suckled her breast while she found him, hard and hot and pulsing, just touching her where he would enter.

But not yet. Not yet. They stroked, caressed,

nipped, suckled until they were both taut and quivering as a stretched bow. Her hands circled him, rubbed him against her. He entered. Slowly. Hard and fiery hot and filling her fully. He wrapped his arms around her, holding her still in his embrace while he kissed her mouth with deep passion.

He pulled himself out, slid in again. Cissy was on fire. His hands braced on either side of her, he stiffened his arms, lifting his weight completely off her. Their only point of contact was where their bodies joined. Slowly he moved in, out, then in again, she lifting her hips with anticipation to meet him each time. He bent his head, suckled a swollen nipple. She feared she would self-destruct, nothing to be found after but a smile.

''Nick...'' She would plead if she had to.

His mouth fastened on hers. She kissed him back hotly, greedily. His weight fell on her as he wrapped his arms around her, holding her to him, carrying her with him as he took her with a fevered urgency to the edge of passion. She wrapped him tight in her own arms, moving with him, her hips rising, her thighs squeezing, mindless once more with only pleasure. Together they fell, together over the edge, his hoarse cry joining hers as they plunged into an abyss of ecstasy.

She clung to him shamelessly, long past caring. He rolled off her, tucked her body into his. The protector. His lips lay against her temple. She heard his even breaths and thought he was sleeping, but then his arms tightened and he pulled her closer to him. She buried her face into the warmth of his chest, allowing herself a few moments' delusion of feeling safe. She'd never been safe. Not where Nick was concerned.

"Cissy." He was the first to speak, the braver of them both.

She rolled away, already too comfortable in his embrace. She glanced over at him. His eyes watched her. An urge to make this easy for him, for them both, filled her as strongly as the passion that had ravished her.

"Well, at least we got that out of our systems." Still her palm went to his strong face, lay on his cheek for too long a moment. The phone rang. She jerked her hand away. He sat up, reached over her, grabbed the phone.

"Fiore."

She watched him openly, wanting even now to touch him, straddle him, take him again. She rolled on her side, buried her face in her pillow, trying to remember the Italian equivalent for "putz." Not that she regretted making love to Nick. What she regretted was falling in love with a man who, like her, had seen the worst paraded as love and had lost faith long before their first kiss.

She listened to the one-sided conversation consisting mainly of "uh-huh," and "okay" from Nick. He clicked off. She felt his welcome weight again as he leaned over her to set the phone back on the bedside stand.

She rolled over and looked up at him. Not a trace

of sleepy satiation remained on his features. His face was hard and set, his lips fused into an implacable, straight line. The Nick she knew and loved.

"You were at the Golden Cue today, right?"

So much for pillow talk. She sat up, pulling the sheet up with her, suddenly too aware of her nakedness. "You know I was. You were having me followed like a politician on the take. Not that I learned anything. You made sure of that, remember?" Back to battle positions.

Nick got up, walked to the closet for a change of clothes. Cissy despised the desire that swelled in her, but boy, she would not mind taking a big bite out of those buns.

Nick pulled on underwear, jeans. Cissy watched in fascination. He turned, stared at her as if waiting for an answer.

"Huh?" Focus, Cissy.

"I asked who you talked to there."

"The bartender. Usually they're Jo Jo's best buds."

"But you didn't find anything out?" Nick pulled a T-shirt with the police department insignia on the pocket over his head.

She shook her head. "Not really. He said Jo Jo used to come in once, twice a week, sit at the bar, have a few drinks until this guy she was meeting showed up. A businessman. Uptown type."

Nick looked up from lacing his sneakers.

"What'd he tell you?" she asked.

He still didn't answer her. He went into the other

room. Grabbing one of his button-down shirts, she put it on and followed him into the main living area.

"Is there a problem, Detective?"

He'd strapped on his gun, cuffs, ID, and didn't answer.

"You're going out?"

He finally looked at her and saw her in his shirt. A flash of smoldering darkness took his gaze. It could have been desire; it could have been anger. "There's a problem. Stay here, understand? Don't leave this apartment. I'll be back."

He grabbed his car keys. He was almost to the door when he stopped, came back to wrap his hand around her neck and pull her to him for a hard, swift kiss. He looked at her unsmiling, tucked a strand of hair behind her ear. He went out the door, slamming it, testing it from the other side to make sure it was locked.

Cissy walked to the door. "That man better stop trying to tell me what to do," she muttered as she slid the bolt into place. But as she leaned against the door, her lips still tingling from Nick's kiss, she knew he was right. She was in real danger now.

Chapter Eleven

Her mother missing. Her sister missing. Phil Lester dead. Jo Jo's boyfriend dead.

Cissy poured a soda, added ice and sat down at the table. Stacks of cash under Cherry's front seat.

She stood, opened the refrigerator, wasn't encouraged. Stared at the fish she was becoming too fond of, chalked it up as displaced attraction to Nick. If she stuck around much longer, she'd be telling him it was time he settled down, started a family. Thirty-two and her mother's genes were kicking in.

She stood, paced from the couch to the fish tank. The sky was only beginning to hint of night, the horizon a red-orange streak that promised more steamy weather tomorrow. The afterglow of hot sex had faded to thoughts of food. She walked back to the kitchen, found a can of honey-roasted peanuts in the cupboard. She grabbed the nuts and the evening paper Nick had thrown unopened on the table and headed to the couch. She spread the paper out on the coffee table. Munching on the nuts, she flipped through the pages, skimming the headlines, too wired to read the small newsprint until she got to the local section. Phil Lester's murder was on the front page. The reporter had taken the fish-out-of-water angle, asking why an unassuming, private man would end up shot and dumped in a motel room.

"Why indeed?" Cissy asked. She thought about the tidy two-story house, the kitchen with checked curtains and the herb garden on the windowsill over the sink. Not exactly a portrait of a pistol-wielding, Harley-riding maniac. Or a man who would end up a corpse-a-gram. Then again, Stevie the Sledgehammer hadn't dropped into Grandview Estates to collect for the March of Dimes. Phil Lester had a secret life.

She flipped to the obituaries. Lester was survived by his mother, predeceased by his father. A younger brother had also died two years ago. Lester had worked for the Department of Taxation. He was also a member of the Table Tennis Association of America. No mention of good ol' Phil's preference for black hogs. Calling hours were from seven to nine tonight at Malone's on Crestwood. Cissy set down the paper, looked at her watch.

Seven-ten.

She should go pay her respects. The man *had* been found in her motel room. And just because she'd slept with Nick, didn't mean she was going to let him tell her what to do.

She shook out the designer suit from her previous life, the one before missing family members and dead bodies and Fiore on the legal side of the law. She dressed, mulling over Phil Lester with his table tennis membership and herb garden and big black Harley. How did he figure into her mother and Jo Jo's disappearances?

Her gut still said Eddie was involved big-time. He was the one the police should be following around—not her.

She slicked Raging Red on her well-kissed lips, smacked them together twice, then wrote across the mirror, Went Out. She had a responsibility not only to herself but to women everywhere to keep Nick Fiore on his toes. She unbolted the door and went out into the night.

She was at the sidewalk before she remembered they were supposed to pick up her rental car when Nick got home today. She'd been so mad about being trailed by a cop, and then…well…she'd been occupied.

The heat had remained hellfire. She calculated the walking distance. She'd never make it without Reeboks. She watched for a taxi and had walked three blocks before one pulled over. She climbed gratefully inside, cursing the masochist who had come up with the idea of pointed-toe shoes.

Malone's receiving room had the velvet brocade furniture mothers used to cover with plastic in the sixties. A few naked lithographs and the parlor could as easily been Madame LaPierre's House of Pleasure. Lester's mother, suffering from the same loss of hair as her son, sat stiffly on a red velvet brocade armchair, dry-eyed and steel-jawed. A few others milled about, conferring in hushed tones. A silver-haired man in a dark suit Cissy assumed was Malone or one of his main henchmen welcomed her with professional graveness. Cissy glanced at the guest book, saw only three other names and was tempted to add her own just so Phil's mother could feel her son did not die without being able to drum up enough people for a decent poker night. But considering the circumstances of their acquaintance, Cissy refrained in a rare nod to good taste.

She went up to the casket and looked down at Lester, a prayer from childhood coming automatically and offered sincerely. Malone had done a good job covering up the bullet wound. Lester's waxy expression was calm, his hands folded across his chest. She finished her prayer, stared down at the dead man as if expecting answers.

She moved to the mother, extended her hand. "Mrs. Lester, I'm sorry for your loss."

The old woman rocked back on her heels, eyed Cissy through slitted lids. "What's your story? You going to claim you're carrying Phil's love child?"

She should have forgone the Raging Red. "Why would you think that?"

"I figure it's only a matter of time. Get in line, sister. Call yourself a lawyer. He left the money to me."

"Money?"

"The innocent act, huh? Is that how you got Phil to play stuff the kielbasa?"

Cissy had to love this dame.

"He was a good boy." Mrs. Lester stared at the

casket, reality sneaking up on the old woman. She looked at Cissy. "How long did you string him on? I'll bet you're in on it. Maybe even the one who offed him."

A gray-haired woman standing to the side came forward, gave Phil's mother a scolding glance, offered her hand to Cissy.

"So nice of you to come. I'm Mrs. Lester's companion."

"Overpriced baby-sitter is more like it." Phil's mother glared at the woman.

"I'm a retired nurse," the other woman told Cissy. "Mrs. Lester's son hired me two years ago."

A full-time caretaker, Cissy thought. On a civil servant's salary.

"Mrs. Lester, I only recently made Phil's acquaintance." Cissy tried to clarify.

"Only takes thirty seconds, as my husband, God rest his soul, liked to say. Listen, girlie, you can pump a whole litter of Lesters out of that carburetor of yours but you won't see a dime of the estate."

Cissy pictured the small two-story in the middle-class development. *Grandview Estates.* Cissy smiled. Mrs. Lester, with her whacked-out frame of reference, must have confused the name of the housing development as her son's residence and decided she was rich.

"More money than you can shake your booty at, babe."

Cissy looked at the caretaker. The other woman's expression was resigned. Nearby Malone nodded with his professional smile. Two people were standing awkwardly by the mint bowl. Malone moved away to greet another arrival.

Cissy tried to get more information from Lester's mother before she had to move on for the next guest. "So, you got the Harley?"

The woman narrowed her eyes. "Why, you a biker chick?"

"No, how 'bout you?"

The woman smiled. "Nah. No one's ridden that Harley since my youngest son, George, died. It was his bike. He restored it, would hardly ride it himself. In the end it was a Pinto that took him out."

The woman's expression turned tragic. "Phil hated motorcycles, but his brother had loved that machine. Phil couldn't bear to part with it. He registered it in his name but never took it out. Scared to death of it."

So much for Cissy's theory that Lester liked to walk on the wild side. Someone else must have been on the Harley yesterday. But who? Lester's murderer? Why had he come after her?

"Phil liked games. He took after me in that respect."

"Games?"

"Games. Cards. Bingo. Parcheesi."

Cissy remembered the computer icons. She thought of Stevie the Sledgehammer and his past employment with the Gambino brothers. "Games of chance?"

"Any game."

"Pool?" It was a long shot but maybe it was a long shot that had taken Lester's life.

"Yeah, he played. But he was no Fats Domino, I'll tell you that."

"I think you mean Minnesota Fats," the caretaker corrected.

"I know what I mean. Take a look at that arrangement there. Look. The one with the big gladiolas."

Cissy knew, in the end, a man is measured by how big his gladiolas are. She turned. Based on what she saw, Lester had achieved the success shared by any man in a mediocre life.

"His friends at the Golden Cue sent that."

"Hello, Candy."

Cissy was digesting Mrs. Lester's revelation when the elderly lady she'd met outside Lester's joined the group. The woman looked at Lester's mother. "This was the hussy at your son's house the other night. She has a key." The woman looked at Mrs. Lester knowingly.

The mother eyed Cissy with new disdain. "We already met."

"Your son must have been a regular at the Golden Cue?" And Otto Chandler must have known him. Had Jo Jo? But the bartender had said the man Jo Jo met had thick brown hair. Lester was bald.

Mrs. Lester was watching her. "Like I told ya, he was no shark. I guess he fancied himself one, though."

Malone, hovering nearby, cleared his throat. Two others had come, were waiting to offer Mrs. Lester their condolences. Cissy touched the old woman's arm. "I'm sorry for your loss."

"Too late to get in on the gold, sister. I've already got my eye on the Armory Bingo Parlor."

"Oh, I like that one," Lester's neighbor interjected.

Lester's mother kept a steely gaze on Cissy. "There won't be a cent left." She crossed her arms over a bosom that had seen better days.

"Nice to meet you," Cissy told the caretaker. "And to see you again." She nodded to Lester's neighbor.

She turned to leave, heard the neighbor whisper, "She's sucking up to you."

Malone met her at the door, thanked her again for coming.

"Do you know the family well?"

"They've always used my services. Are you a relative?"

"A recent acquaintance. You did a nice job on him, considering."

Malone narrowed his eyes, giving his face a ferret-like look.

"The wound," Cissy whispered as if sharing a secret.

Malone's sharp expression relaxed. "I tried. Mrs. Lester wasn't too happy. Said the deceased wore a hairpiece that made him look like a snake-oil salesman but she'd grown used to it."

Lester wore a toupee. *Dark brown. Thick. Kennedy hair.*

"You didn't use it?"

"No one could find it."

"Couldn't find it?"

"Between you and I, it would have made my job a lot easier."

Cissy looked at Mrs. Lester. "Is she all right?"

"Senile dementia, I understand. I'm not sure she really realizes what is going on."

"She wants to buy a bingo parlor."

"Gambling." The funeral director nodded wisely. "That's where the real money is."

Cissy glanced at the casket. "Can't beat the odds on death."

She stepped onto the porch. At the rail, a man stood smoking. He turned as she came out, appraising her. He nodded.

"Shame about Lester." She sidled up to the man, glad she'd worn heels. Undoubtedly the sisters at St. Anne's had been right on the money when they'd caught her and Dee Dee Crocco giggling in the girl's room, high on sacramental wine. Cissy would burn in hell one day. But for now, she wanted information.

The man nodded again. "He was all right. Trying at least."

Now Cissy studied the man. "You work with him?"

The man shook his head, stubbed his cigarette into an urn filled with sand. "Friend."

Cissy took a random shot. "Shame about the... well, you know."

The man cut her a glance, tapped another cigarette out of the pack. "Got to give him credit though. Took him a while but he got it out of his system. Had a bad spell after his brother's death but eventually he worked it out. Wouldn't even buy a lottery ticket. Now this.'' He lit his cigarette. ''Makes you wonder.''

Cissy adopted a thoughtful expression. ''Sure does.''

''That's where I met him—G.A. He sponsored me. Wish I could say I had the success he did.'' He took a drag on his cigarette. ''How 'bout we have a few drinks in Lester's honor?''

First time she'd been hit on at a funeral. Not that she had any right to judge, snooping for info before the interment had begun.

''Quite an accomplishment, Lester kicking his gambling problem, huh?''

The man nodded, cautious now that she hadn't responded to his offer.

''He sure did run up some big bills at the bookies in his day though, didn't he?''

The man blew out a stream of smoke, eyed her through the haze. ''How 'bout that drink?''

The man wasn't giving it away. Neither was she.

She declined and left. Two blocks away, she cursed herself for not calling a cab from the funeral home. At the third block, she decided to hobble back. If it was a choice between hammer toes or fending off horny gamblers, there was no contest.

She turned around, had gone back a half block when a dark sedan pulled up beside her. Nick rolled down the window and took her in, flamenco heels, discreet peek-a-boo slit in the skirt, silk camisole beneath the light jacket. He didn't bother to conceal the desire in his dark eyes. The rest of him didn't look happy, however. "Get in."

She rounded the car as he leaned over and opened the door for her. She slid into the seat. "Do you have me wired?"

He pulled out into traffic. "The old lady from Grandview Estates called the station. Said she had a hot lead on the Lester case. Said the woman who tried to break in to Lester's house just left the funeral home and she overheard you were after Lester's money." He had the nerve to smile.

"I went there hoping to get some clue how Lester fit in with my mother's and sister's disappearances. And to pay my respects."

Nick shot her a skeptical look.

"I said a prayer," she told him.

"For who?"

"Lester. He could just be an innocent victim in this mess."

"Don't go soft on me now, Spagnola."

She stared at his take-no-crap profile. He was right. One multiple orgasm and she was Mary Poppins.

"Lester's mom is a whack job. Senile dementia."

Nick nodded. "Yeah, we interviewed her."

"She accused me of carrying Lester's love child."

"Are you?"

"You're a laugh riot, Fiore."

He cracked a grin. She turned away, struck always by how beautiful he was. But now something more than animal lust took her breath. A deeper need. Scrappy Cissy. Always had to play with the big boys.

"Lester's mother does have a round-the-clock private duty nurse. Phil was footing the bill for years."

"Met her, too."

So far, she'd been scooped.

"He must have made a healthy salary to support round-the-clock care for his mother." She paused for flair. "Plus a gambling habit."

Nick shot her a look, surprise coming and going in a blink. "Our sources say he beat it years ago."

"So does his buddy from Gamblers Anonymous. But his mother claims Lester left her a rich old woman. Guess she won't be crazy anymore. Just eccentric."

"Lester had a little money put away in a savings account, a few bonds, company 401K. The house is half paid for but it's hardly enough for an upgrade from crazy to eccentric."

"She's already planning to become a bingo mogul."

"So maybe he was lucky. Stashed some money away from his winnings. Invested it in her name. Or maybe he fell off the wagon but didn't want to let anyone know, figured he could control it, stop before it became a problem again. Except he couldn't stop and Stevie the Sledgehammer was brought in to correct it."

"Why'd they dump him in my room, then? And what about Easy Rider yesterday afternoon?"

Nick was silent.

"The Golden Cue sent him a big spray."

She'd gotten Nick's interest. She liked it.

"Anything else?"

"He wore a rug. Only—"

Nick glanced at her.

"No one can find it."

"That's it?"

"Come on, tell me that doesn't get your detective juices flowing. The bartender at the Golden Cue said the man Jo Jo was meeting had a full head of hair. It had to be Lester."

Nick turned the car into the police station's parking lot, turned off the engine.

"What are we doing here?" She smiled big Raging Red lips. "It's the toupee tip, isn't it? I just broke the case."

Nick turned to her. It was the combination of concern and confusion that frightened her.

"What's going on?" She hated the plea in her tone. He reached out to take her hand. She pulled it away. "Don't patronize me, Fiore. Tell me what's going on?"

"We need to ask you a few questions."

"About what?"

"The bartender at the Golden Cue."

"Why?"

"You were one of the last ones to see him alive."

Chapter Twelve

She wished she had given him her hand.

"He was found in the Dumpster behind the Golden Cue. One shot to the middle of the forehead. A .22. They found a coaster with your number on him."

She turned her head to the window, soundlessly gulping oxygen like one of Fiore's fish. On a fish it was amusing; on a woman, pathetic. The blast of oxygen to her brain set off a buzzing. Colored dots began to mambo before her eyes.

"There was no sign of a struggle."

She blinked away the dancing dots, schooled her face strong and turned, the thrum of blood hard at her temples.

"Whoever it was, the bartender knew his murderer. Or the guy's a good shot."

"Same bullet as Lester and Jo Jo's boyfriend?" Focusing on details would keep her calm, take away the thought that a man she'd spoken to this afternoon was no more. He had probably still been wearing his arm garters.

"Results aren't back from the lab yet, but my

money says it's the same gun, a .22. It does the job without making a big mess.''

''What'd you learn from Fat Eddie's robbery report? What kind of gun did he have?''

Nick gave her a long look. ''A .22.''

''So he's a suspect, right?''

''We're watching him.''

''Jo Jo knew all three of the victims. Now she and my mother are missing.''

Nick said nothing, but she could read his thoughts. His cop thoughts. *Or they're dead.* Time and multiple murders were against them. She was grateful to Nick for not saying it. Nick Fiore had a sensitive side. The surprises just kept coming.

They got out of the car. Nick took her elbow in a firm hold. It could have been a gesture of support or an attempt at control. With Nick, it was a toss-up. After sleeping with the man, Cissy knew better than to speculate.

Nick led her to a room with a long table, introduced her to two other officers. One had a notepad in front of him. The other was angled back in his chair, his hands resting on the beginnings of a belly that unchecked, could cause him trouble passing the police physical in later years. Nick introduced her and remained standing while she took the indicated seat. He leaned against the wall, arms folded, cop face on.

The officer with the belly dropped his chair to all fours. ''You went to the Golden Cue around 1:00 p.m. today, Miss Spagnola?''

''That's correct.'' She sounded good. Lawyerly.

"Call me Cissy." She was on her best downtown behavior. The cop taking notes scribbled something on the pad.

"Why?"

"My sister, Jo Jo, has been missing for several days. My mother, too."

"We know." The officer had been trained not to show sympathy. She was glad.

"My sister's last place of employment said someone saw her hanging out at the Golden Cue. I was hoping maybe someone there might be able to give me some information, something that would help me learn what happened to my sister, my mother. People don't just drop out of sight."

The one cop looked up from his notepad. His bland gaze skewered her. *Sure they did,* it said. For a rare moment in her life, she knew what it was like to be the naive one.

"Did you learn anything useful?" the other detective asked.

She told them what the bartender had told her about Jo Jo and her mystery date. "He didn't really know anything. That's why I don't understand why..." She looked at the wall.

"Maybe he knew more than he told you."

In the cop's tone she heard the same "Back off, baby" Nick had used when he'd told her to let him do his job.

"Bartenders don't usually talk," the detective continued. "They listen."

"You're right. This one wasn't chatty," she said,

glancing up at Nick. His face stayed clean of expression. "But I was feeling generous, and he was feeling gregarious."

"You gave him money?"

"I tipped him well."

"How well?"

"I had a spring water with lemon. I left him sixty dollars."

The cop opposite her looked to the one with the notepad. "He had his wallet, right?"

His partner flipped back several pages. "Wallet was in his back pants pocket. No money."

Cissy leaned forward. "He was robbed," she said as if she was a fellow investigator.

The cop with the paperwork shook his head. "Still had all his credit cards, ATM cards."

"Too risky," Cissy theorized. "Easily traceable." She might have joined the force.

The cop who had done the questioning stared at her flatly. "Thank you, Cissy, for coming in. If you think of anything else, have Detective Fiore contact us." He pushed back from the table. The other policeman picked up the pad and pen.

"That's it?"

The policeman with the middle-age midriff stood, looked down at her. "Unless you have something else you neglected to tell us?"

Both officers stared her down. She almost smiled. She'd been winning stare-offs since parochial school. Staring down a cop was nothing compared to staring down a nun.

"My mother has been missing for two days, and to my knowledge, no one's seen my sister either."

"The report says your mother left your father."

"Stepfather. That's his story. I'm not buying it."

"There's no evidence to the contrary...yet."

"Three men are dead."

"All leads are being investigated."

"My sister dated Saint-Sault. She knew Chandler, and the man she was meeting at the Golden Cue was Lester, except he wore a toupee." She leaned forward. "A toupee that's missing. His mother wanted it on him for the viewing, but no one could find it."

"Someone killed him for his hairpiece?" the detective deadpanned. The other detective's lips tightened as if suppressing a smile.

Cissy ignored their amusement. "All three victims were killed by a .22. Eddie reported a .22 stolen."

"Ma'am, we need more than circumstantial evidence. Be assured the investigation is ongoing, and we're working on several leads."

Cissy became alert. "Such as?"

The detective's glance at Nick said, *Keep a leash on this one.*

"We'll keep you apprised if there are any new developments." The detectives headed toward the door.

"Find my mother and sister. That's the only development I need to be apprised of," Cissy told their retreating backs. She shifted her gaze to Nick, still leaning against the wall.

"Smooth, Spagnola."

She stood and strutted out of the room without

waiting for him. Anger had always been her balm for anxiety and a smart-aleck attitude preferable to tears. Rationalization didn't prevent her from slamming the car door.

Nick opened the door, looked down at her with a calm she envied. Of course, anger management was probably a required course at the Academy for ex-hoodlums.

"I'm not scared of you, Spagnola."

"Bull. You're frightened as hell."

It was his soft low laugh that made her wish he'd pull her up into his arms and kiss the fear out of her. He closed the door. She sighed as he rounded the front of the vehicle, even though she knew she'd survived a close one.

He slid into the car, started the engine.

"I want to go pick up my rental at Lester's." Snotty now.

He put the car into gear, his silence allowing her attitude. Probably figured three dead bodies and two missing were worth a snotgram or two. They drove the twenty-minute ride to Grandview Estates without talking, like an old married couple. The rental was where she'd left it on the far edge of Lester's lawn. Nick pulled up behind it, the motor idling. They both stared at the dark house.

"The police searched the house thoroughly, right?"

He sent her a dry look. "Don't get any ideas. They didn't find anything. Neither will you."

"It doesn't hurt to double check." She pulled back

the door handle. "What about the rug? It's still missing." She was beginning to feel better.

"If you go near that house, I'll have to arrest you."

She gauged his seriousness.

"Tampering with the scene of a criminal investigation."

He was serious. She looked at the house. So was she.

"Listen, Lester's gambling got out of hand and he got mixed up in something he shouldn't have," Nick tried to persuade her.

"Except he hadn't gambled for two years."

"Put that on his gravestone."

Cissy stared at the house, then glanced at Nick. She had already admitted to herself she hadn't a chance in the strange, wondrous war between them. That status wasn't about to change. He would arrest her if she went into house.

She pushed open the car door. "All right. I'll meet you back at the apartment."

"What about dinner? Provenza's serves until ten and it has private booths in the back. It's quiet there."

She knew what he meant—safe. Dinner in an almost deserted restaurant, she, dolled-up in her best pay - your - respects - to - the - man - found - murdered-in - your - motel - room outfit. Nick under low lights that turned his Italian heritage lethal. Saltimbocca and tiramisu. Nick was wrong. Dinner at Provenza's was far from safe.

She shrugged. "Meet you there." She had a death wish.

He waited for her to pull out first. She glanced in the rearview mirror. He was right behind her. "Sheesh, sleep with the guy, and we're joined at the bumpers." She was fiddling with the radio, trying to find a station, when her cell phone rang. She glanced in the mirror, saw Nick on her tail. The phone kept ringing. She snatched it out of her purse, tucked it to her far ear, fluffing her hair to conceal it.

"Spagnola."

"Cissy?"

The connection wasn't good. The voice was female and for a moment, Cissy's heart rose. "Mama?"

"No, it's me, Pauline from the bar."

"Oh." She heard sorrow in the syllable.

"You gave me your card yesterday."

"Yes?"

Pauline paused. Cissy's interest spiked. "Yes?" she urged again.

"Well, I like my job here, ya know. I mean it beats cleaning out rat cages over at the research farm. And on Thursday and Friday nights, the tips triple most weeks."

"Sure, I understand." El simpatico.

"So, when you and the cop came in yesterday—"

Cissy glanced into the rearview mirror, saw Nick's fatal gaze. Steering with her knees, she waggled a wave with her free hand to offset suspicion.

"Well, I didn't want to say anything. I didn't want to get in trouble, but I liked your mother. She was good to me—always let me have the heavy-tip nights, said she didn't need the money, but, hell, you and I both know that's a lie. Who doesn't need money?''

Cissy thought of the stacks of cash she'd found in the Thunderbird.

''I didn't want to get in any trouble. But I keep thinking about the nuns.''

''The nuns?''

''Shoot, I wish I'd had a camera the afternoon they come walking in. Two-for-one had just started. I got so nervous I asked them if I could get them a round of Virgin Marys.''

''Nuns can do that to you,'' Cissy agreed solemnly.

''They were looking for your mother. She was in the back, prepping the kitchen. I got her and brought her out. The nuns start telling her that they had appreciated her generous donation so much, they just felt it wouldn't be right if they didn't come by and tell her in person and how much good the money will do and on and on, and all the time, your mother is shaking her head, saying, no, any pleasure it brings to you and the good work of your order can't compare to the joy it's given me to be able to share it with you.''

''It must have been quite a large donation.''

''That seemed the gist of it. No figures were thrown around—''

No, nuns weren't tacky.

''—but those nuns were sure gushing over your mother.''

Gushing nuns. Something you don't see everyday.

''I wouldn't be surprised if they nominated your

mother for sainthood. And from their conversation, I got the impression this order wasn't the only one your mother had donated to. They kept talking of her other 'good works' with other orders.''

Where was her mother getting large amounts of cash to support nuns across America?

''What order was this?''

''Sisters of the Sacred Heart, on the other side of the river.''

''What did Eddie think of this?''

''Oh, Eddie wasn't there, and your mother asked me to keep this between ourselves. Said Eddie wouldn't much cotton to the idea of nuns hanging out at the bar. Customers didn't want to be reminded of Sunday morning on a Saturday night.''

''Sounds like Eddie might not have known about my mother's charitable activities?''

''I don't know. I figure every woman deserves to have her secrets, right? Especially since Eddie had some of his own, not quite so admirable ones. That's why I called you. I'm not one hundred percent certain but, well, I think he was having an affair.''

Cissy cursed him righteously.

''I overheard him bragging one day to a customer. Said the woman, whoever it was, was crazy about him.''

''The man's delusional.''

''Hey, love is blind, ya know.''

''Deaf and dumb too, obviously.'' She looked in her car mirror, smiled big at Nick, turned her head slightly so he couldn't see her moving mouth.

"Your mother never talked about it, but I got the sense she knew something was going on. I think that's why he bought the house a few months ago. After that he had it made. Your mother tucked away out there, his mistress in town, the business which gave him an excuse for late nights, sudden emergencies."

Was that why her mother had been working more hours? She'd known Eddie was fooling around and wanted to keep an eye on him?

"When I heard your mother was missing, well, it just doesn't seem right."

"No, it doesn't."

"Then today…"

"What, Pauline?"

"Eddie was talking to a lawyer on the phone. He was asking how long it'd take for a divorce to go through when the other spouse was missing."

"What?" Cissy almost ran a stop sign. "Not wasting any time, is he? Do you know what lawyer he called?"

"No."

"If you find out or hear anything else that could be helpful, you'll call me, won't you, Pauline?"

"I'll try."

"Are you at the bar now?"

"No, it was slow so I knocked off early. Manny said he'd close."

"Is Eddie at the bar?"

"He was in earlier for a little while, but like I said, it was slow. He left about the same time I did. Said he was going to go home, have a few cold ones, watch the Mets game.''

As if he didn't have a care in the world. Why would he? If Louisa ''disappeared,'' his problems were solved. He got his freedom, his business, the house, and his mistress. She clenched the steering wheel.

''Pauline, thank you again for calling me.''

''Your mama was a good woman.''

Is a good woman, Cissy silently corrected. ''I'll make sure no one knows where this info came from.''

''I appreciate that.''

''And if you think of anything else, I'd be grateful if you gave me a call.''

She said goodbye, disconnected and furtively slid the phone down and into her handbag. She'd suspected Eddie from the start. Finally she had a motive. Now she needed evidence. Solid evidence that wouldn't be dismissed as circumstantial by the police. And what about her sister? And the murders of the other men?

Watching Nick in the mirror, she grabbed her phone, speed-dialed Eddie's number, again tucking the phone against her left ear where it couldn't be seen. She didn't even know what she was going to say. The answering machine picked up. A new message played in Eddie's voice. Her mother's voice had been erased. Cissy's hands trembled.

They were almost at the restaurant. She blinked fast, banishing any tears, and pressed down on the accelerator. She pulled into the outer lane, passing a car. Nick stayed tight on her fender. The light turned red at the intersection, forcing her to stop. A glance showed her Nick's pissed-off countenance.

"Sorry, sweetheart." The light still red, she pounced on the gas, swerving the car left into the oncoming traffic. She barely avoided being broadsided by an oncoming taxi and a Volvo in the opposite double lanes. She saw the cab driver's mouth working, knew whatever imaginative epithets he aimed at her, they didn't compare to the names Nick was calling her now.

She heard the siren that would stop the other cars to give Nick the right of way. She had only a few seconds' head start. Tires squealing, she made another turn and another, slowing down only enough to avoid losing control on the corners. She gritted her teeth. "I hate driving. I hate driving."

But when she glanced in the mirror, she didn't see Nick. So far, she'd lost him. She took another turn toward the arterial when she realized Nick had probably already alerted his patrol buddies. She'd be stopped before she got to the interstate's on-ramp. She turned toward the longer but less traveled—and hopefully less patrolled—river road. After ten minutes and no sign of Nick, she called him.

"I'm sorry," she said. "I'm going to have to take a rain check on dinner. Something came up." She pulled the phone away from her ear in anticipation of his response. All she heard was a curious silence. That was worse. She put the phone back to her ear. "Nick?"

"You're not supposed to talk on a cell phone while driving a vehicle." He was mining for information.

"That's only if the vehicle is moving, right?" Two could play this game. "Listen, I'll explain everything later when I get home." *Home?* "Don't worry about me."

"I don't."

"Yes, you do." And she was beginning to get used to it. She disconnected and turned the phone off.

Her mother and stepfather's house was dark when she pulled up, the surrounding woods equally shadowed and thick. "A nice, quiet spot," her mother had told her. Another time Cissy would have appreciated the solitude but tonight the isolation held no comfort. The sun had set but the darkness wasn't deep yet, the world a gray-black. An uneasy time, ripe for images sooner forgotten. The hour when fears gathered their strength, readied to spin out long and hard and wrap around the unwary.

Despite what Pauline had said, Eddie's Mercury wasn't in the drive. Cissy didn't know if she was glad or disappointed. She'd sped out of the city in the mood to confront, the frustration of inaction and lack of progress spurring her on. The car's high speeds had helped to release some anxiety and promote the return of rational thought. She now realized she had no idea what she had hoped to accomplish by racing out here. She studied the house. No signs of life. She should go back, but to what? She had an image of Nick waiting with the handcuffs, and not for the purpose of fulfilling her fantasies. She pulled off the private road, concealing the car in a stand of trees on the outer edge of the property. She turned off the engine, studied the house. She shoved her purse out of sight under the seat, got out and locked the car. Hell, she never could say no to a dare.

She figured the front door would be locked but checked its handle, new and shiny, anyway. She went around to the back. It was unlocked. Country living.

She knocked as she opened the door on the chance someone was in the house. "Hello? Eddie?"

It was quiet, too quiet. She squinted hard, making the shadows into shapes. The walls were bare studs, wires hanging, the room, like the rest of the house, in a state of renovation. She pulled out the cupboard drawers, looking for the junk drawer her mother always kept. She found it, second drawer from the bottom in the cupboard next to the refrigerator. She rummaged through it until she found the flashlight her mother always kept there. As a child, Cissy had always kept one under her bed, too. Nights when Eddie had come home unable to get his key in the door's lock, and the arguing had started and the yelling became too loud, Jo Jo would sneak into Cissy's bed. They would burrow under the covers, Cissy would turn on the light and pretend they were in a tent camping somewhere far away. She'd tell her little sister stories, sing her soft songs.

She clicked the flashlight on, swept it across the room, not knowing where to start, looking for something, anything that could link Eddie to her mother and sister's disappearance. The supposedly stolen gun would be a definite bonus.

She crossed the room, staying close to the studs and the new Formica countertop. The kitchen led into where a wall had been knocked out to form one large open space with the living room. A wide-screen TV dominated one wall, a sectional with a recliner at either end curved around the adjoining room.

"Eddie?" Cissy called out now just to crack the quiet. Her voice sounded as small as it had been those nights under the bedcovers.

The rooms circled back into the kitchen, the stairs to the second floor in-between. She had her foot on the first step when she spied the door to the cellar.

Too cliché. But since when was Eddie a genius? She pulled open the cellar door. The light switch was near the door but she didn't click it on. Too risky. She went halfway down the stairs, swept the light into the room. The basement had the stone walls and dirt floor and low ceiling found in eighteenth-century houses. She went down another two steps, moving the light into corners, up walls. She didn't know what she was looking for. She couldn't even think the word "body" yet.

She went all the way down the stairs. The light swept the room, sent the insects skittering. The damp scent and musky air gave the room an unholy feeling.

She walked the floor, patting the dirt with her toes, looking for recently turned soil. She poked the light into some boxes stacked on a metal shelf, old luggage shoved in a corner. On a wooden counter, cords and hoses were jumbled. Splattered paint cans sat on the floor underneath. A narrow doorway led to a small space for the furnace. Except for the usual basement disarray, nothing looked out of the ordinary. She started toward the stairs and the rest of the house waiting to be searched.

Scurrying sounds near her feet caused her to stop. She snapped the light to the floor in front of her. Supersleuthing or not, no way was she stepping on the soft, furry middle of a fat rat. The light shone a small circle on the dirt floor. Nothing. She flashed the light across the floor. Nothing but damp dirt and a smell like a high school boys' locker room. She swung the light's beam like a saber as she continued across the floor and up the stairs. She was almost to the cellar door when she heard a click, another door swing open. She stopped. Her heart slammed into her chest. Someone had come home.

Chapter Thirteen

She pressed hard on the flashlight's switch, pushed slowly to prevent a click. Darkness now. Blind, she pressed herself to the wall, the stair rail cutting across her lower back. The house was old, settled. The cellar door had swung closed, except for the latch hitting the frame. She stretched out her arm toward the door handle, grasped it when the kitchen light came on. Her hand shot back as if burnt. She froze, stared desperately at the door, listened to the sounds so near in the kitchen. Afraid the ajar door would be noticed and she discovered, she crept down the stairs, the end of her big toe tapping silently like a divining wand, finding the surface of each step. She winced each time a step protested.

"Eddie?"

A woman's voice called as Cissy had done. Only this voice was playful, promising.

"Eddie? What'd you do? Go to bed already? I told you I'd only be an hour or so."

Pauline had been right. There was another woman. The floor above Cissy creaked. She tiptoed down the last steps toward dark corners. She heard cupboard doors opening, closing. *That is my mother's kitchen,* she thought with a strange sense of crazy. *Get out, harlot.* Harlot? She'd never anticipated having opportunity to use *that* one. If it wasn't for her current predicament, she would have laughed. A hysterical laugh.

The harlot was humming. Sounds above Cissy's head told her the woman was moving into the large living room. The television came on. Cissy had to get out. She glanced up at the door, outlined by the kitchen light left on. Her big toe tapped against the dirt floor.

Steps above her head returned to the kitchen. Cissy heard the clatter of dishes being put into the sink. Her mother had talked about the new porcelain sinks in so many different colors but in the end, she'd chosen stainless steel because of the price. Always practical, her mother. Except when it came to men.

The light around the door dimmed. A fainter light, probably the small bulb in the new stove hood that matched the appliances, had replaced overhead lights. A perfect night-light so someone who might want a snack or to sneak out of the house wouldn't hurt themselves. Quite considerate, actually.

Footsteps headed back to the front room. The television stayed on. It was only a short sprint from the cellar door to the back one. She could creep up the steps, tiptoe across the kitchen, out the back door. The television would cover any noises. She waited for her eyes to adjust to the new darkness, started toward the steps, her hands stretched out in front of her, feeling her way.

She was on the second stair from the top when footsteps came into the kitchen. She stopped, paralyzed. The footsteps crossed the kitchen, came down the hall, past the cellar door. Light swelled along the door's outline again, then vanished as another door closed. Cissy stood, motionless. A toilet flushed. The water ran in the pipes past her, imitating the blood rushing in her head. A door opened, footsteps heading back to the kitchen. A hand automatically pulling on the ajar cellar door as it passed. The door shut tight.

Don't lock it. Don't lock it. Cissy prayed, shamelessly reverting to childhood beliefs. A hesitation. The woman on the other side of the door surely heard Cissy's heart banging in her chest. The bolt slid along the door's top. Cissy could almost hear the gods laughing. The footsteps moved away, not that it mattered anymore. Cissy stood for minutes, staring, the fine muscles that controlled her bladder clenched in spasm. She grasped the door handle, squeezed her face into a hard walnut. Bracing her arm, she pressed down on the door handle to be sure. She held her breath, pushed. No movement. She was locked in Fat Eddie's cellar.

No more soft glow around the door now. Only darkness. The smell of damp dirt; the heavy humidity hoping to make stone sweat. Above, the sounds of the television. She clicked the flashlight on boldly now, sliced its beam around her current cell. As she started down the steps, the flashlight's beam grew dim. She shut the light off, waited until her eyes adjusted before going farther. At the bottom of the steps, she switched the flashlight on long enough to look for the least cobwebbed corner. None of the areas she scanned seemed to be in the running. The light wavered. She turned it off, stepped toward the metal shelves, switched the flashlight on as she poked among the gathered odds and ends, hoping for batteries.

The light sputtered. She turned it off, could do no more than grope blindly. Her hand touched something unidentifiable except for the term ''gross.'' She jumped, swallowed the yelp that almost sounded and decided then and there, she was as lousy a detective as she had been a stockbroker. She snapped on the dim light to see the cause of her distress was only a crusted chamois.

The light flickered, wasn't going to last much longer. She searched the shelves, hoping to find batteries or another flashlight. The light sputtered, then died. She clicked it off and on in a panic. Nothing.

She felt her way back to the staircase, brushed off the bottom step with her hand and plopped down. She listened for skittering sounds and was rewarded. She drew her legs to her chest, wrapped her arms around her calves and banged her forehead against her knees. She couldn't stay locked in this cellar all night. There had to be a way out.

She waited, hoping the flashlight, if left off, would charge, give light. After several seconds of nothing more than the sounds of television and the night noises old houses make that give rise to ghost stories, she clicked the flashlight. Nothing. Well, she couldn't just sit there. She stood and, using her hands and what night vision was possible in the complete darkness, she felt her way along the wall, the hard perimeter making her escape impossible until suddenly it yielded. Cissy stretched her arms, waved her hands but felt only air. She walked into the darkness, slammed into what felt like a metal wall. She felt the barrier, realized she was only in the narrow space off the cellar's main room that stored the furnace. She followed the metal shape, finding nothing but a stone wall on the other side. She used it to circle back to the main room when it ended. Stretching her arms, she felt only air. She stepped forward and yelped as she stubbed her toe on something hard and solid. She clamped her hand over her mouth, listened keenly for sounds upstairs signaling she had been heard. The television droned on but had been joined by the sweetest sound Cissy thought she'd ever heard. The nasal ripple of snores.

She bent down, her hands reaching to find what had stopped her. She felt a narrow, raised rough surface. A step. Her hands flew across it to find another and another above that. She climbed the first step, the next. On the third step, her head thudded on something hard above. Her hands flew up, found the smooth surface of metal slanting down. Midway along its length her fingers stopped, clutched a latch. She smiled. An outside access door.

She stiffened her arm, pulled the latch down so not

to make a sound. The click came, deafening to her ears. Holding her breath, she pushed on the door with a tight resistance to prevent squeaks. The slightest scrape and she stopped, hoping the sound would be attributed to the house settling.

Halfway up, the door protested with a whine rivaling that of a fourteen-year-old girl. Cissy didn't care. She'd seen the sky above. She pushed and climbed the five steps to freedom. At the top, she lowered the door with the same care she'd used to open it and stood triumphant, one foot splayed on the angled door, hands on hips, as if she'd just discovered new territory. She headed toward the lawn's edge and her car when she stopped short. Something at the property's perimeter, where the woods began, moved. She stood still and exposed in the backyard and stared into the night. New sweat thickened on her upper lip. Out in the darkness, she stared into the shine of eyes.

Fear clutched her. Her mother gone. Her sister missing. Three men with bullet holes in their bodies. Was it her turn? She stared into the night, thinking of her mother and her sister and steak saltimbocca and Nick. Two glassy orbs reflected moonlight and calm. Patience. A killer with his weapon of choice and the solitude of land and night had no reason to hurry. He could wait, savor the moment, enjoy the wondrous swell of excitement like a first erection. While the voices babbled inside his mind, grew louder, stronger, silenced only by a shot, a slice, a strangulation.

And she, center stage, not knowing if she should

run or stay still—either way it seemed her fate would follow the others. Which would displease the monster more? That she would not flee but come toward him as if to embrace, of course. She stepped toward the trees.

The leaves rustled. A deer stepped into the clearing, stared at her. The deer who came out of the woods, ate out of her mother's palm. The animal stared at her unblinking, this woman so overrun with relief, her body weaved in the windless night. He took a step.

She stared into those reflective, questioning eyes. "I know, buddy," she said too softly for the deer to hear. "I'm looking for her, too." Cissy's throat felt like it was closing, the clutch of breath before tears.

The deer blinked several times, circled toward the woods, looked back once as if to see if Cissy was following him. Those woods, too, held secrets. The deer disappeared between the trees. Too many secrets, unanswered questions. Cissy took a step, but no more. She would come back another time, in the day's heavy heat and hard light. Now she would go to her car. Her body was weary and wanting to sit, sleep. She thought of Nick's skin, his scent, his strength. She suddenly had no more strength. She stood, not sure if she could move beyond this day, this night. She took a step.

A woman's scream split the darkness. Sanity shattered.

The wail came and came, crying out as if the night had read Cissy's thoughts and sounded in sympathy. She whirled to the scream's direction. The house. A light upstairs. In the window was a woman, her head fallen back as if too heavy to hold up, her mouth open in a spiraling howl so primal, Cissy almost envied her release. She froze, fighting the compulsion to join in as a dog hears the howl of another and responds. Raise her face to the moon and let loose for what was no more and what never could be. She was running to the house now, stumbling up the steps, crashing through the back door, toward that one light, that noise, that noise, not knowing what she would find, what she would do. Only knowing she had to stop the scream.

She pushed open the door, the air conditioner in the window blowing full blast, causing her to step back. So cold. The room's muted light softened the other woman's silhouette. Her shoulders hunched, her fingers clawed at her cheeks, her bellows simmered into hiccuping sobs. Eddie lay stretched out on the bed, his hands folded across his bare chest in a rare posture of patience. The covers were loosely arranged across his belly's full rise. He might have been waiting, anticipating his mistress and the delights of night. A bullet hole in his forehead had come first.

The mistress turned, saw Cissy. Her scream was enough to wake the dead. Cissy glanced at Eddie. Hadn't worked.

Cissy held up her hands to show no harm.

"What the hell are you doing here?" The mistress backed away, her hands patting the air behind her, flailing for something heavy, solid, a suitable skull-cracker.

"What the hell are *you* doing here?"

The classic "a good defense is a good offense."

"Better yet." She nodded toward Eddie. "What the hell happened to him?"

"The man's dead. Have a little respect."

Cissy looked down at the body. She examined her feelings as she examined the dead man. She thought of the rocky past, her missing mother, the man she'd believed responsible now turning up dead before a jury could hang him. No justice in this big, bad world.

She'd never wish Eddie dead. It's just there had been too many times she hadn't wished him alive. She looked at the other woman, meant in the most literal of terms. The woman glared back at her. She was at that meanest of ages when there was only enough prettiness left in the face to remember what used to be. The rest was yearning flesh, skin that caught her tears and caked her makeup into its folds.

"I'll go call the police." Cissy meant Nick.

As she turned toward the stairs, she glanced out the window and saw a dark sedan pull up. Nick had found her. Unchecked relief came, so rich it would make her do and say crazy things if she wasn't careful.

"Detective Nick Fiore just pulled in."

The other woman didn't seem to hear her. She was looking at Eddie. Her breath caught in a hiccup. Her eyes were puffy. Enough makeup had been washed into the cracks in her face to make Cissy believe she'd really cared about Fat Eddie.

"I'll go and let the detective in."

The woman stared at Eddie and sighed. The loose skin on her upper arms jiggled.

"Did you want to stay up here with…him?" Cissy asked lamely.

The woman looked at Cissy with black-mascara smeared eyes. She really was a mess. Corpses could do that to a person.

"Thank you. I'm Rogina. Rogina Krauss."

"I know who you are."

The woman's eyes were the eyes of the street. "I know who you are, too."

As long as they understood each other. Cissy headed out the room to face Nick.

"SAINT-SAULT, Lester, the bartender at the Golden Cue, Eddie. What's the connection?" Most men paced as they thought out loud. Nick didn't pace. He didn't even prop one foot on the kitchen chair or twist it around with one hand and straddle it. A little disappointing on that last one. One thickly muscled arm crossed over the other and his body made a slight curve against the counter. That was it. Nick leaned. That was all that was necessary. Toughness wasn't an act with him. It just was.

"Bullet holes." Nick's question had been rhetorical but Cissy had felt the compulsion to answer. She needed more than a lean to look tough—more like an Uzi, but what she lacked in size and strength, she made up for with attitude. It generally worked.

"And you."

He didn't even point an accusing finger. So much

for brute force that under other circumstances might have been the beginning of a good sexual day-dream…or a porno film.

"I'm under suspicion big-time, aren't I?"

"Everybody's under suspicion."

She didn't know if he was playing with her or not, purposefully keeping it light. He'd insisted on sitting in while the police had played twenty questions with her as well as Rogina down the hall. Rogina hadn't given them any answers. Said Eddie had picked her up, brought her to the house for fun and games. She'd used his car to run back into town to meet a girlfriend, have a drink. She came home about two hours later and found Eddie. Claimed she knew nothing about Cissy's mom's disappearance except the story Eddie had fed her. Yes, she had been pressuring Eddie to divorce his wife. He'd told her things weren't that simple.

Yeah, this was a community property state, Cissy had thought. Half the house, half the business. Still if Eddie had told her mother he wanted a divorce, he probably hadn't expected a fight. Why should he? Louisa had never fought back before. *Oh, Mama.*

Cissy tried for the same tidy alibi as Rogina. She said she'd heard Eddie had filed for divorce, went to the house to talk to him. She'd been angry, yes, she admitted in response to the officer's questions. The house was dark when she got there. She thought no one was home. Decided to take a look around. Even to her own ears, it sounded flimsy. To cops that had heard more lies than ladies' night in a singles bar, it put her at the top of the suspect list. But with no evidence linking her to Eddie's death, plus one of their own taking her home, the cops could only promise they'd be keeping an eye on her.

Nick, too, had been watching her closely since he'd arrived on the scene. Once she had glimpsed worry in his eyes and realized it was concern, not suspicion, that was responsible for his attention. Four bodies in three days. Her mother and sister still missing. Behind his scrutiny he was waiting for her to crack. He should know better. Still, she appreciated the thought. Made her feel too tender toward him. She'd come out of this thing one way or another. Barely intact, perhaps, but she'd survive.

He gave her another one of those killer perusals. She could have been on suicide watch. Too late. She'd already slept with him. And wanted to again. Pure suicide.

"You don't think I killed Eddie?"

"No, but my perspective has been skewered."

"That's your way of telling me you're madly in love with me, isn't it?"

He didn't even blanch. He was tougher than she thought.

"Your first day back, someone tries to scare you out of town—"

"It wasn't Lester. At the funeral, his mother said he never rode the bike. It was left to him by his brother who died a few years ago. He kept it around for sentimental reasons."

"I knew that from her interview."

"You got any more secrets, Fiore?"

He smiled and scored an easy one. Attitude couldn't hold a cannoli to raw sexuality.

"Lester would have taken the Hyundai to take me out."

He shifted to the opposite side, smiled as if he knew she was having a sexual fantasy about him right now. Heck, just having him three feet in front of her was enough to get the juices cranking.

"So it wasn't Lester on the bike. Just in my motel room." Back to business.

"Scare tactic. Somebody wants you out of the way."

"They also wanted Lester, Saint-Sault, Chandler and now Eddie out of the way."

"No, whoever it is, if he wanted you dead, you've given him ample opportunity. Someone wants to scare you, not kill you."

"That's a comfort."

"Your mother and sister are missing. Someone decides you shouldn't be in town either. You go looking for Lester. He winds up dead in your motel room. You go talk to Chandler at the Golden Cue. He winds up in the Dumpster. You go snooping around Eddie's. He's dead in bed."

She giggled. Nick's gaze was on her. It was two in the morning. She'd cleaned out the entire supply of jujube fruits in the station house's vending machine. Several cups of cop coffee guaranteed she might not sleep until the next century. She'd been questioned about a dead body for the third time in two days. Nick was right to watch her closely. Gallows humor was the only thing that stood between her and the scream that wouldn't stop.

"What about Saint-Sault? He was in that trunk before I came to town. You can't blame that one on me."

"I'm not blaming anything on you. I'm looking for connections here."

"I was so sure Eddie was the one responsible for Mama and Jo Jo's disappearance."

"He very well could have been, but whatever happened, it's more complicated than a spat between a husband and wife. Too many people involved. Lester, I think he got in over his head—"

Cissy's synapses started snapping with that last statement. "What about Lester's hairpiece?"

Nick stared at her.

"Don't you think it's strange no one can find it?"

"Only you. Four people are dead because of a hairpiece?" A corner of his mouth quirked.

"No. I'm just saying…" She really didn't know what she was saying. It was late and the world had stopped making sense several days ago.

Nick shifted, sending her equilibrium spiraling. "Then there's Jo Jo," he said.

"What about her?"

"Like you said at the station, she was Saint-Sault's girlfriend, used to meet Lester at the Golden Cue, chatted it up with Chandler. Whatever's going on, she's involved."

''But what about my mother? What's she got to do with this?''

Nick shook his head. ''I don't know if we'll get that answer until we find her.''

She knew every hour that passed, every corpse found put the possibility of her mother and sister being alive at greater odds.

''That's all I've been trying to do,'' she told him.

''Me, too, Cissy.''

''What about Stevie the Sledgehammer?''

''We're still looking. He's connected but no one's talking yet.''

Connections. Deeds had them. So did the cops. She needed them, too. She thought of Tommy Marcus.

''You've got a gleam in your eye, Spagnola.''

Damn cops and their observational powers. ''Maybe I'm hot for your bod—''

''No 'maybe' about it.'' He smiled quickly before his face turned stern again. ''We've got too many bodies piling up for you to be playing Dick Tracy.''

He was right. What he didn't understand and what she'd never admit was she'd racked up too many failures in the past fifteen years. If she failed now, the consequences would be absolute.

''Don't get gentle with me now,'' she told him, dead serious. ''It'll put me over the edge.''

''C'mon, you need some sleep.'' He moved toward her with the grace of a man in control. He took her hand, pulled her up to him and kissed her with a sweetness that stung. He led her to the bedroom door, took her in a strong embrace that tested everything Cissy believed about their relationship.

"Hey," she murmured against the hard rock of his chest, struggling for survival even as her hands found his wide shoulders and held on too tight. "I thought you said I should sleep."

"You will…"

He smiled. So did she.

"Eventually."

Chapter Fourteen

She woke with his body wrapped around hers and, for the first five minutes of the new day, she wasn't afraid. Then reality reared its pointy head. She rolled away from Nick's heat. When he woke, she was propped on one elbow, studying him.

"You snore in your sleep," she told him.

"You drool."

She smiled. He smiled back. That's how things had always been between them. Simple.

He got up in one smooth, swift motion, one of those people who woke instantly.

"What's on your agenda today?" he called from the bathroom.

She stretched under the sheets. "The usual. Have a little breakfast, read the paper, catch a killer."

He came out of the bathroom, a towel wrapped around his waist and a warning in his eyes. "Why don't you give my sister a call? Catch up on old times?"

"Nice try."

"I promised you I'd find your mother and Jo Jo,

Cissy. Crime lab is going over the evidence found at the scenes. I'm going to rattle a few doors today, see what I can find. There's nothing you can do.''

She had actually been feeling amorous until that last line. She swung her legs over the side of the bed and stood. ''You never learn, do you, Fiore?'' She headed past him into the bathroom.

''What the hell is that?''

''What?'' She craned her neck over her shoulder.

''This.'' Nick squatted, traced a finger down the back of her calf to the small hollow of her ankle, short-circuiting her efforts to be annoyed with him.

She looked down. The small bandage had come off while she slept. ''It's a tattoo,'' she snapped. ''They're very fashionable nowadays.''

''What's it supposed to be?'' His finger drew a large circle around the image.

''It's the ancient Chinese symbol for 'long life.'''

His low laughter came from behind her. His finger circled the image again and again, then moved back up, tracing the curve of her calf, skimming the length of her thigh, reaching between her legs, finding her moist and warm, the intimate folds of her body parting to wrap around his finger in invitation. Then his hands held her hips. His lips, his tongue found the swell of her backside. A sexual heat shot through her, damning her. The fine skin across her chest flushed pale rose. When he turned her, she feared her legs would weaken, her body buckle, but his hands held her. Her support. Her strength. He nuzzled her, found her hot and moist. Lying would not save her now. A whimper released as he suckled her. She did not know for what she pleaded. She took his head in her hands while his tongue swirled for long seconds. The swell inside her mounted, gathering layer on layer, spreading so that she grabbed his shoulders and her thighs trembled. The death she had seen the past two days filled her. She cried out, the violence inside her now. Her head snapped back. Her body arched. Her nails dug into the firm flesh of Nick's shoulders.

He eased away slowly as if regretting leaving. His hands stayed curved to her hips. She drew him up to her, placed her mouth on his, tasting him, tasting herself. She wrapped her arms around his neck, pulled him closer, not caring that she clung too tight. Death could make you do crazy things like that.

His hands cupped her buttocks, lifting her so her legs wrapped around his hips. Her back braced the wall. Their bodies joined, her hips splaying wider from the force of him, opening, asking him to fill her until all she would know was him. He thrust deeper, harder. Her muscles clenched around him. Air rushed from her chest. She opened her mouth in release only to have him cover it. She sounded her pleasure inside him.

After, they stood, his weight warm on her, she flat to the wall, any bold victory brief. He kissed her once more, hard and intent, but there was tenderness in the hand he curved to her cheek.

The kiss ended. ''Thank you,'' she told him.

Hardness settled behind his eyes, betraying the desire that still took his features. "Don't thank me. I'm not a kind guy."

They'd both played the act so long, the lines rolled off their tongues easily. "I'm not thanking you for your kindness."

He stared down at her as if he'd finally met his match and wasn't happy about it. She flattened her hands on his chest and pushed him away. He smiled, grateful.

"You're a freaking cream puff, Fiore." She walked into the bedroom.

He showered, dressed, met her in the kitchen where she'd started the coffee. She got up to fill her cup as he came in. She'd thrown on one of his button-down shirts and nothing else, just to see him squirm. She wasn't disappointed.

He filled a coffee cup and sat down. "You going to behave yourself today?"

"What do you think?"

"I think you'll do as you damn well please."

She clinked her coffee cup to his.

"Cissy."

He looked too serious. She was good with comebacks and hanging tough, hot, sweaty sex and long moments entwined. But seriousness, at least with Nick, was something else. She wasn't sure how to handle it. In fact, the entire scenario, him dressed for work, she making coffee, sharing a cup together as the day began, was a little too Ozzie and Harriet for her. She and Nick didn't do that shtick. So far, she'd avoided trying to figure out what was happening here between them. She'd had murder and missing family members to occupy her. But dressed in his shirt, the scent and strength of him flagrantly surrounding her, and him across the table looking solemn as if someone had just died. Which someone had, of course, but—

The phone rang, interrupting her thoughts. Nick got up and answered it. "She's right here." He handed the phone to her.

She took it with a questioning look.

"Tommy Marcus," he told her.

"Hello, Tommy." She'd left a message with his service last night for him to call her in the morning. She was ready to take him up on his offer to help.

"Cissy, I got your message. I also just heard about your father on the morning news."

"Stepfather." She was being petty, but death had done little to temper her feelings about Eddie.

"Yes, right. Do the police have any ideas how this could have happened? Or why?"

"They're investigating now." She watched Nick go into the other room.

"Awful. Any word on your mother, your sister?"

"No, not yet, but it's only been two days."

"Yes, of course." Tommy reassured her, masking any doubt.

"Listen," he said, "what can I do? How can I help? You probably want to postpone the funeral or at least the burial until your mother returns."

"Yes." Cissy confirmed the fact her mother would return. "I'll be talking to the funeral home today, but

I called you because I remembered you said maybe, with your connections—''

''Anything, Cissy. Anything. Listen, you've had a heck of a couple days. How 'bout we meet for lunch at La Serre? Get your mind off things. We can discuss everything then and I'll see what I can do.''

She hesitated. Nick came into the room, ready for work. ''All right, Tommy. Yes. Maybe that's just what I need.''

''Great. Shall I pick you up?''

''Why don't I meet you there? Twelve-thirty?''

''Perfect. I'll have my secretary call for reservations.''

Cissy hung up, met Nick's gaze. ''I'm having lunch with Tommy at La Serre today.''

''Good.'' He strapped on his gun belt. ''At least I know you'll be out of trouble for two hours.''

''Not necessarily.''

He lifted an eyebrow. ''Trying to make me jealous, Spagnola?''

Embarrassed, she realized it was exactly what she had been trying to do. ''Don't you have to go save the world?''

''Nope. Just the city. Come here.'' He drew her up into his arms, kissed her hard on the mouth. He looked down into her eyes which were beginning to focus again.

''Go see my sister.''

''Go save the city.''

''You're beginning to really bug me, Spagnola.''

''Don't sweet-talk me, Fiore.''

Their smiles met, then their mouths. Her earlier assessment had been wishful thinking. Whatever was going on between them, there was nothing simple about it.

SHE HAD TAKEN a shower, was standing in the middle of the bedroom naked when she realized she had nothing to wear. Her sweaty suit from last night lay in a crumpled heap on the carpet. She dressed in the pair of shorts she'd bought her first day back, rummaged through Nick's bureau drawers and found a T-shirt much too big for her. She got her wallet and sat down on the bed, emptying its contents. She had to have one credit card that wasn't at its limit. She pawed through the plastic squares. She'd only had one that hadn't been maxed out when she'd arrived, but the car rental would take care of that. She propped her chin on her hand. The money she'd found stuffed in between Cherry's cushions was gone, except for a twenty. Her first unemployment check should be waiting when she got back to New York. She could borrow a little of the money she'd stashed in the safety deposit box yesterday, pay her mother back once she cashed her check. She stacked the useless plastic cards. She should cut them up. She slid them back into her wallet. She was brave but, like the cards, she had her limits.

The phone rang as she headed out. It was Al's Auto Palace, telling her the car was ready whenever she wanted to pick it up.

"How much?" Her brow furrowed as she heard the answer. "Any discount for cash payments?"

Pleased by the answer, she mentally added it to her loan and told Al she'd be over this morning.

She went to the bank, counted out a thousand dollars in a private room, fanning the money in front of her. She replaced the bundles and left. The day's heat was already searing. She headed to Al's Auto Palace, dropping off her rental on the way.

"You were lucky. I was able to call around the junkyards and find a fender for that particular year's model," Al told her. "Had to charge you extra, though."

"I understand." Cissy peeled off twenties. Her hands were sweating, the cash sticking together. She rubbed her hands on her shorts.

"Spoke to Hank over at Auto Restoration and was able to match the paint. Custom color, though. That cost you, too."

Cissy continued peeling off twenties. She smiled at the man with the grizzled beard and the warm quart of beer, one-third empty on the counter behind him.

She left the top down as she pulled out of Al's, although it didn't help beneath the climbing sun. She headed toward the mall, sweating in the hot breeze but happy to have the Thunderbird back. She turned on the radio loud to drown out her thoughts and pressed on the gas, letting the speed and the sun and the new morning convince her everything would be all right. Repeated glances in her rearview mirror showed no unmarked sedans or masked motorcyclists.

She arrived at the mall, hot and thirsty, and bought a bottle of water. She made her purchases and headed back to the parking lot, its asphalt spongy from the heat. In the car, she took out the money she'd "borrowed," counted what was left as she drank the rest of the bottled water.

She went back to Nick's to change. She twisted her hair into a topknot and planned to put the convertible's top up on the way to the restaurant. The open windows would still have their way with her, but at least she wouldn't look as if she'd just emerged from a wind tunnel when she met Tommy. She got to the restaurant twenty minutes early, more than ready for air-conditioning and a cold drink.

She told the hostess she was meeting someone and went into the lounge to wait. She ordered a water with lemon, tipped the waitress when she brought it and stuck the rest of the cash on the table beneath her glass.

She took a handful of peanuts from the bowl in the table's center, watching the noon news on the television suspended over the bar. She frowned at the slight stain on her fingertips as she was about to pop a few peanuts into her mouth. Her hands must have been damp or the ink must have been wet on the newspaper she'd scanned at Al's this morning while she waited for him to bring the car around. She picked up a cocktail napkin, dampened it with the condensation on the outside of her glass and rubbed her fingertips.

She half listened to the weather report promising

hot, hot and more hot, and ignored the sports report. She glanced at the clock. The news was almost over. She watched the door while the broadcaster promised they'd be right back with an interesting follow-up to a story reported yesterday on counterfeit bills being found in Wisconsin. Several people came into the restaurant, but no sign of Tommy yet.

''Nuns with funny money,'' the waitress commented as she came up to see if she could get Cissy anything else. ''Now I've heard it all.''

''What?'' Cissy turned her attention away from the door.

''Just on the news now.'' The waitress tipped her head toward the television. ''Counterfeit money found in the Midwest was traced back to grocery store purchases made by a local convent for their community soup kitchen.'' Shaking her head, the waitress walked over to another table.

Nuns with funny money. Cissy rubbed her fingertips together, studying them. She slid out the five-dollar bill the waitress had brought from beneath her glass. She wet her fingertips on the outside of the glass, rubbed the five between her fingers. She took the bill away. No stain.

She fumbled in her purse for her wallet, pulled out a twenty she'd taken from the safety deposit box this morning. She wet her fingertips again, rubbed the bill. She looked at her fingers. No stain.

''Cissy?''

She jumped, not having noticed Tommy had come in.

"I didn't mean to startle you." He glanced at the bills littering the table. "Our table's ready if you are."

"Yes, let me just get my things here." She picked up the change from her twenty, the other twenty still in her hand. She stopped, the bills in either hand. She rubbed them between her fingers, the texture of the twenty different, its weight thinner, its grain slicker. She shoved the money inside her purse.

"I'm going to stop at the ladies' room a moment. Why don't you get our table and I'll meet you there."

His eyes studied her as he returned her smile. "Sure."

Cissy slipped into the ladies' room, dropped her purse on the counter beneath a wall mirror and opened her wallet, her hands sweating now, and not from heat. She felt the other twenties, compared them to the ten and five the waitress had brought her. She wet her fingers, rubbed the other bills. Again, no stain. She smoothed her fingertips across the lone twenty still crinkled from being stuffed in the car's seat cushions. She pulled her hand away, saw her fingers had darkened. She wet her index finger again, rubbed the tip hard over the twenty's surface. She pulled it away, her skin darker.

She stared down at the bill, heard Pauline's voice. *I keep thinking about the nuns... They were looking for your mother. Start telling her how much they appreciated her generous donation.*

Cissy gathered the money, real and fake, off the

counter, shoved it in her purse and went into the dining room.

"Tommy, I'm sorry." She ignored the chair he'd pulled out for her. "Something's come up. I can't stay for lunch."

Tommy's expression darkened with concern. "Cissy, what is it? Is something wrong?"

She shook her head. "I'll call you. I'm sorry." She rushed out of the restaurant, pulling her cell phone and a worthless twenty out of her purse and dialed information as she walked toward the Thunderbird parked two blocks down. She asked for the number and address she needed, writing them down in reverse on the counterfeit bill—an old memory trick she'd learned in high school. From one of the nuns.

"Sisters of the Sacred Heart."

"This is Cissy Spagnola."

"Yes, how can I help you?"

"I believe you already have." Cissy slid into Cherry, started the engine. "I'd like to speak to my mother or sister, please?"

"I'm sorry? Are they members of the order?"

Just her luck. A nun who didn't crack. "Ask Jo Jo who got into a hair-pulling match when I found out she ripped up my poster of Menudo."

She didn't know whether the silence at the other end was a good sign or not.

"Please?" she pleaded as she pulled out into traffic.

"One moment."

Cissy said a prayer aloud while she waited. Finally the sister returned on the line.

"Jo Jo said she's sorry she ripped up your Menundo poster."

Cissy blinked back the tears, blurring the traffic. "Tell her I'm sorry, too. Tell her everything's going to be okay." Something nudged her side. Thinking her gym-bag-sized purse had slid, she absently pushed at the annoyance. Her hand landed on something solid. She looked down to see a gun stuck into her side. The hand that held it had an upside-down cross tattooed on the inside of its wrist.

"Now tell her," Big Bill's voice came from the back seat, "we want what she has or you die."

Chapter Fifteen

"Are you there?" The nun at the other end of the line waited for Cissy to answer.

Cissy glanced down at the gun shoved into her side. It had been the hottest part of the day. The car was parked in plain sight on the street. She'd left it unlocked, the windows down. "Hello? Hello?" she said as if she couldn't hear the nun on the other end.

"I'm right here, Miss Spagnola."

"I'm sorry, I can't hear you." She shook the phone. "My phone must have died." She heard a disgusted sigh from behind her.

"Give me the phone," Big Bill growled.

"I can hear you perfectly, dear," the nun said at the other end of the line. "Are you in some kind of trouble?"

"Give me the phone." The gun went deeper into her flesh.

"Yes, yes." Cissy answered both the nun and the bum in the back seat. She felt a new pressure at the base of the seat.

"That's a 9 mm at your back to make sure you

behave.'' The other gun left her side. The hand came back empty, grabbed the phone.

"Tell Jo Jo we're done playing games. Either she gets everything we need to us by tonight or she'll be telling her sister she's sorry for a lot more than ripping up some poster. What? What's that? You're going to pray for me?''

A nun they couldn't crack. And Cissy had thought she could hang tough.

"You pray that Jo Jo gets us what we need or we'll all be saying prayers for her and big sis.''

Cissy heard the phone click. She reached out for it.

She heard a chuckle. " 'Scrappy Cissy.' "

"The bitch of it is I genuinely liked you, Big Bill. So what's the plan? Kill me like you killed the others?'' As she chattered, she searched for ways she could draw attention to the car. Emergency flashers had a distinctive, repetitive tick. Big Bill would notice them right away.

"Take a left at the corner, get on the interstate.''

"Bodies have been piling up faster than seventy-five-cent pitcher night since I've come home. No wonder you're getting a little testy.''

"So don't aggravate me.'' The gun burrowed into her rib cage again. The pressure at the base of her spine stayed strong.

"What kind of gun is that?'' Cissy indicated the pistol at her side. "A .22?''

"A .22? That's a girly gun. This is a .38 Special. Designed to take care of business.''

So Big Bill wasn't the killer. All the victims had been killed with a "girly" gun.

"What has Jo Jo got that you need?"

"Don't worry about what Jo Jo has. You just worry that she gets it to us."

"Counterfeiting is a change from the Lords' usual crimes. What, they expanded their horizons in prison?"

"Thought I told you not to aggravate me."

"What does Jo Jo have? Evidence on the operation? Did she take the account books? The printing plates?"

Big Bill gave a mean chuckle. "Printing plates? This is the computer age, doll. Nobody uses presses."

She thought of the computer equipment she'd seen in Lester's house. "So Lester's hobby was more than printing neighborhood fliers. But how'd he get hooked up with the Lords?"

"He didn't. He wasn't working for us."

"So that's why you killed him."

"We haven't killed nobody...yet."

"Tell that to the county morgue."

"Listen, I'm telling you the Lords had nothing to do with those murders."

"I'd like to believe you, Big Bill, but I find that hard to do with a gun shoved in my side."

"If anybody killed anybody, it was the southern network. They're the ones who moved in while my brothers were behind bars."

"Is that who Saint-Sault worked for?"

"In the beginning. Mainly running drugs, but he

was small-time. He came into the port, learned that with the Lords put away the local operation wasn't going to make it much longer and saw an opportunity. The southern organization had been looking to expand their territory. They pounced on the ring, brought in the money and muscle, organized access to the ships. Ba-da-bing. The operation's international.''

''But then the Lords start getting released.''

''And nobody was too happy to find their turf taken over. Saint-Sault was pissed off by this time, too, felt he'd practically put the ring in the southern boys' laps only to be overlooked. The southern boys knew Saint-Sault used, and they didn't like it. Drugs make a man unreliable. So Saint-Sault starts feeding information to the Lords, and Jo Jo starts working Lester, trying to find out more about the organization. Who the main associate was in the area that was calling the shots.''

''So the southern network could have killed Saint-Sault. Did they think Lester was working with Saint-Sault and kill him, too?'' Cissy wondered.

''Maybe. Somebody was working both sides. Somebody had tipped off the southern network about the New Orleans raid. Not long after that, Saint-Sault is found This Side Up.''

''So, say the southern boys had him killed. Jo Jo gets spooked, not knowing if Saint-Sault talked or not about her pumping Lester. She goes into hiding.''

''Jo Jo was spooked, all right. She calls Eddie, tells him she's got everything to shut the southern boys down and put the Lords back into power. The price is two million dollars.''

''Money no one was planning on paying her.''

''Hey, the chick's a garbage head, but she's got stones, you gotta give her that. Eddie told the Lords not to worry. He'd take care of it. He still owed them for a favor they did for him a while back.''

Cissy thought of the bar bombing and Nick's cousin. ''He should burn in hell.''

''Nice way to talk about family.''

''He wasn't family.'' But Louisa and Jo Jo were, and she had to save them. Not to mention her own skinny butt.

''What about the bartender at the Golden Cue?''

''Listen, I ain't got all your answers. The fun and games have gone on too long.''

''So that's what threatening me and sticking a body in my room was? Fun and games?''

''Your sister isn't too steady to begin with. By now she's got the shingles. Any police involvement and the deal was off. So what do you do? Come into town and climb into bed with Nick.''

''I'm staying with him temporarily for my own safety.''

Big Bill chuckled. ''You'd think a guy who can 'cha-cha' like that could control his women.''

Cissy gritted her teeth. ''So the Lords didn't kill Lester, just stuck the body in my room. Tell that one to a jury.''

''Pure luck there. Stevie Deed was looking to get in good with the Lords, knew it was only a matter of time before they'd be controlling the port again, so he volunteers to go to Lester's, shake him up. When he gets there, he finds Lester already dead. He gives us a call. We're trying to figure out what to do about you. Stevie says he'll take the bike out for a spin, give you a little scare. We tell him not to kill you— Jo Jo might not like that.''

''So Stevie tried to scare me on the Harley, but it didn't work.''

''You'd think you'd get the message.''

''Scrappy Cissy.''

Big Bill chuckled again. ''So Eddie told Stevie to stick the body in your motel room.''

''Then who killed Lester?''

''I'd say somebody who didn't want him talking.''

''When Stevie found the body, was Lester wearing a toupee?''

''Yeah, he wore a rug,'' Big Bill's voice was amused. ''Stevie said the thing must have fell off when he moved the body. Only, he was in such a hurry, he didn't notice it until he'd dropped off the body and was heading to the tavern to tell Eddie and Manny. The piece was on the floor of the front seat. Stevie thought the damn thing was a wild animal. Scared him half to death. He almost shot it.'' Big Bill laughed. ''He chucked it in the Dumpster when he got to the bar. Get off at the exit after this one. Take a left off the ramp.''

Cissy reviewed her options. Big Bill had the gun, but she had the wheel of an easily recognizable hot red Thunderbird.

"After you take a left, turn right at the second light, and go about three blocks to Olive Street. You'll see a brick warehouse with a white truck in front of it. Pull into the drive and park around the back."

Cissy breezed by the exit.

The gun rammed into her side. "What the hell are you doing?"

"Go ahead. Shoot me. I'm doing seventy. If you're lucky you'll die on impact."

The man chuckled. "You're a real firecracker, Cissy. Too bad we didn't meet again under more pleasant circumstances."

"You're a real snake charmer yourself, Big Bill." She pressed down on the gas pedal.

"I almost hate the idea of having to kill you."

"I'm not fond of the idea myself, but at least I shaved my legs this morning. Go ahead. Kill the driver of a car going seventy, wait, seventy-five, eighty coming at ya, and see who walks away alive."

Silence told her she had him thinking. Still crouching low, he pushed his upper body between the seats, reached his arm across her lap.

"What the hell—"

The gun that had been at her back was now shoved in her side. Big Bill wedged the other one between her thighs, its snout on her left kneecap. "This leg here isn't doing much but looking pretty now, is it? One shot to the knee. It won't even be missed."

He moved the gun up her body until the barrel rested on her left elbow. The other gun stayed hard in her side. "Then again, nobody needs two hands to drive, either. I say there's all kinds of body parts we could eliminate.'' He aimed the gun back on her knee. "One by one.'' The gun went to her left elbow again. "Here a shot, there a shot.'' The gun moved to her knee, back and forth, back and forth. "Everywhere a bang-bang. Which will it be first?'' He rested the gun on her leg. "Knee?'' He slid the gun up. "Elbow? Lady's choice.''

She slowed to seventy, sixty-five. Her cell rang, causing them both to jump. The man swore. Her last stunt hadn't succeeded, but it had rattled him.

"My phone is ringing.''

"Let it ring.'' With two guns pressed against her body, he raised his head enough to see out the front window without being seen out the back. "Get off at the next exit and turn around unless you want hamburger where your left kneecap used to be.''

She knew that look. It was the look Eddie had when he'd come home from a hard night's drinking. It was the look her first husband had when he broke her jaw. She looked for the next exit.

Big Bill punched in a number on her cell phone. "Yeah, we're on our way. Few minutes more. We took a little detour. We're turning around at the next exit. Yeah, you know, this broad's a piece of work. I'm ready to kill her just to relieve some stress.'' He listened, gave a low laugh. "Yeah, yeah, I know there's other ways to relieve stress.'' His gun circled her knee, slid down her calf, caught the hem of her skirt. The cool point of the gun moved up past her knee, raising the skirt, exposing her thigh. She slapped it away, pulled her skirt down and shot Big Bill a dirty look. Inside she trembled.

Big Bill snickered. "Yeah, right, okay. I'll do that and meet you there."

Her one advantage gone, Cissy focused again on some way to draw notice to the car. She searched the console for an answer.

Big Bill hung up. "Okay, give it some gas, sweetheart."

She glanced at the gas gauge. It was below Empty. She suppressed a smile and pressed on the gas. "You're the boss."

They drove in silence, guns wedged to Cissy's body. She checked the gauge several times. She could smell her captor, herself. The ripe smell of terror.

"Where are we going?"

"I told you, brick house. Olive Street. White truck."

"What's the white truck for?

"You."

She glanced at the gauge. She had no idea how long the car would go before it ran out of gas. "You guys are making this unnecessarily complicated, you know."

"Life is complicated, Cissy." His gun absently traced up and down her thigh.

"You don't have to kidnap me. I know where my sister is. Just force me to take you there."

Silence. She had Big Bill thinking.

"Make you kind of a hero to the big boys, wouldn't it?"

"You'd never give Jo Jo up," Big Bill decided. "Take this exit."

Cissy did as he said.

"Now turn around there and get back on the interstate," Big Bill instructed.

"Four people dead, and you get the goods without even a scratch. You'd be a legend."

"Keep driving."

"Because it seems to me, they have you doing the grunt work right now. Say you and I get pulled over. Who's going to get hauled downtown or end up a cop killer? Not your buddies. No, they're probably lying around right now, sucking down a cold one, watching the best of Jerry Springer. Why not, when they've got guys like you out in broad daylight, hauling bodies, kidnapping a cop's girl," she added just for fun. "Stevie already had his butt hauled in the other night. Four are dead. Who's next?"

"You if you don't shut up."

She thought of the sunken-chest beanpole boy getting his butt kicked up and down the block. "Just seems to me like you're still letting the big guys push you around, that's all, Billy."

"Nobody is pushing me around."

"Get the goods, and you won't be just another babbo."

"I ain't no babbo."

"Nah, you're just the chump on the front line that will go down first. Think they'll come visit you when you're doing twenty to life?"

He wiggled the gun in her ribs. "And I should trust you?"

"No, you shouldn't trust me, Billy. You shouldn't trust your buddies waiting at the van. You should trust yourself. Trust your instincts. That's what all the great ones go on. Instinct." She'd been lousy picking stocks, but she could sell the hell out of them. She glanced at the gas gauge.

"You are a piece of work, Spagnola. I'm actually going to regret it if they do kill you."

She glanced at him. He smiled. "Head to Olive Street and step on it. We've already wasted enough time."

Her foot pressed all the way down on the gas pedal, but the car didn't pick up speed. It was losing power. She smiled back at Big Bill. The car slowed. She scanned the highway. They'd left the city, had headed to the suburbs. Off the shoulder, the land dipped steeply, then rose again and rolled into a line of trees hiding the interstate from a housing development.

"I told you to step on it."

"I am."

He glanced at her foot on the floor, looked at the gauge, uttered a profanity.

The car slowed quickly. She steered it to the shoulder of the road and let it roll.

"Ya know what's funny. It's not the big things that trip guys like you up. It's the little things. Stopped for a busted taillight, only to find a body in the trunk. A serial killer pulled over for unpaid tickets and confesses to twelve murders. A car runs out of gas during a kidnapping.''

The car stopped dead. She stuck it in Park. Her other hand grasped the door handle. It was now or never while Big Bill was still trying to understand how such a minor detail could bring him down. Her elbow came back swiftly, catching him on the bridge of his nose. She heard a delicious crack. She grabbed the car keys, jammed them into his baby blues. The gun at her knee went off, but the blow had angled it upward, shattering the glass. She rolled out of the car, crawled underneath. She'd never reach the trees. She heard Big Bill getting out, cursing her and her future generations. She was counting on him assuming she'd gone over the guardrails. Two feet hit the asphalt, looking very large and mean in heavy black work boots.

''I know you're under there, Spagnola. Five cars are coming. As soon as they pass, you'll be dead, doll. One…two…three…four…say a prayer, sweet—''

A thud. Big Bill hit the pavement, stared at her as surprised as she. He didn't blink. Neither did she. He didn't breathe. Neither did she. He was dead. She wasn't.

''Cissy?''

She closed her eyes, letting the sound of her name in Nick's voice wash over her. She wanted to cry. With joy. With sorrow. She didn't know. She didn't care. She'd come too close this time to pretend she didn't love this man. She turned her head, saw his face. Fat, shameless tears outed her every emotion.

"Nick?"

"Yes?" His voice was careful.

"I really, really hate driving."

He didn't smile. Her tears had scared him. She took his offered hand, eased out from under the car, swiped at her wet, dirty face.

"Detective Jones and I were on our way to the Lords' clubhouse when I saw the Thunderbird go by. I knew you were supposed to be meeting Tommy for lunch. I called the restaurant and Tommy said you'd left in a big hurry. When you didn't answer your cell phone, I suspected something was wrong."

She didn't know when he'd put his arm around her or started leading her gently to the car. All she knew was she was grateful for him. His colleague stood over Big Bill's body.

"I'm not going to lose you now, Cissy," Nick said in a low voice.

She looked at him, but his gaze was straight ahead, not inviting additional comment. The sun beat down on them both. *Tell him,* the nagging voice inside her demanded. *Tell him you don't want him to lose you.* She looked at his hard profile. *Say something.*

She stopped. "Nick." He turned, looked down at her. She hesitated. The opportunity passed.

"My mother and sister. I know where they are. They're alive."

"Where?"

"The Sisters of the Sacred Heart."

Nick rubbed one side of his head.

"Amen," Cissy said.

Chapter Sixteen

The building was clapboard and unassuming. A wooden sign nailed near the door read Sisters of the Sacred Heart. A woman with a bare face and short, severe hair answered the door. Only a heavy carved cross on her reined-in bosom signaled she was of the faith. Cissy knew traditional habits were no longer mandatory at many orders today. Still, something about a nun in street clothes never failed to shock her.

"Sister?" Her voice turned pious. Her early religious indoctrination might not have been successful, but it had had an effect.

"May I help you?" The woman's gaze flickered to Nick, back to Cissy with general interest.

"I'm Cissy Spagnola." Recognition sparked in the woman's expression. "This is Detective Nick Fiore. We called. We're looking for my mother and sister. I pray we've come to the right place."

The woman smiled the most blessed smile Cissy had ever seen. She vowed right then and there to go to church every Sunday and to give up white sugar and wine during Lent and give more to the homeless.

She was still seeking ways to repay God as the sister stepped back from the door. "Please come in." She led them down a long hall to the back of the house. Along the way they passed several nuns, some in street clothes like their hostess, others in blue habits.

"Your sister and mother are waiting for you in the prayer garden. It is secluded, designed for the sisters to worship in private. No one can see from the outside. It is safe. Your mother is a good, generous woman." She looked at Cissy, her expression grave. "We have tried to help your sister. We have not yet been successful."

Cissy's heart sank. What had she expected? A miracle. *People don't change that much, Spagnola.*

"She had no drugs when she came here. But she has since found sources."

"How?" Cissy asked.

"Your sister is very resourceful when circumstance demands it. We have made it clear she is welcome to stay, but she must be willing to work through her problems. We can offer her counseling, sanctuary, but the choice must be hers. It is now, as always, in God's hands."

They walked down a trail intersecting well-tended gardens until they came to a group of close-standing pines. "Behind the pines you will find the garden's entrance. Your mother and sister wait for you there." She turned to Cissy. "God bless you both." She moved toward the house. Cissy and Nick started toward the pines.

She saw Jo Jo first, too thin, frail, beaten by much

more than bad men and bad money. Her mother rose. Cissy went to her arms first, but when the time came for her to embrace her sister, she held on to her tighter, longer, as if afraid Jo Jo would slide out of her arms and slip away. Afraid she already had.

"We didn't mean to involve you, Cissy." Her mother sat down as if tired. Cissy saw the ivory rosary wrapped in her hands, the tiny beads her mother's hands worried. "We called, tried to tell you to stay away, but we couldn't reach you. Then we were afraid if we contacted you, and they found out, they'd try and get it out of you. Jo Jo made it clear to Eddie that if anything happened to you, the deal was off, but who knew with these animals?"

Cissy sat beside her mother. "I'm fine, Mama. Relatively." She smiled, squeezed her mother's rosary-laced hands.

"If you had called once in a while and given me your new phone number all this could have been avoided."

Cissy glanced at Jo Jo, and in the silent language between two sisters conveyed, *Can you believe her?*

Jo Jo rolled her eyes. "Try being cooped up with her and a bunch of nuns for three days."

"Don't get me started on you, missy," her mother warned.

Cissy's smile widened involuntarily. She patted her mother's hands. "It's good to be home, Mama." She meant it.

Her mother's features softened. "It's good to see you, Cissy."

"How did you find us anyway?" Jo Jo asked.

Cissy explained how Pauline had mentioned the nuns coming to the bar, the news item on a nun in Colorado passing counterfeit cash.

Her mother sighed. "I didn't even know it was counterfeit until Jo Jo told me the other day. All I knew was over the years Eddie always had his secret stash but now I find too much money. No good comes from too much money. I don't want no harm to come to him. He was a bastard, yes, but he was my husband. I married him. So, I figure I make a deal with God. I send the money to the sisters so they can take something bad and do something good with it. Some run shelters, offer protection to abused women. The money will do good. Except now I find out it's counterfeit." Her fingers worked the rosary beads. "I'll never be able to show my face in St. James again."

"C'mon, Ma." Cissy patted her mother's shoulder. "God's got to have a sense of humor."

Jo Jo looked at Nick. "You guys find out who killed Jacques yet?"

Nick had stayed back, letting the women have their reunion. He stepped forward. "Thought you might be able to help us with that, Jo Jo."

She shook her head.

"More have died."

Cissy took her mother's hands in hers again, rosary beads and all, and held tight. "Mama, you know Eddie's dead."

She saw her mother's features crumble, then realign into a strong mask. "I read it in the paper," her

mother said flatly. She looked ahead. There were no
tears. Her mother had learned long ago her tears could
be a sign of victory to another. She would not give
her abuser the satisfaction. Then or now.

"You didn't make any arrangements yet, did
you?" she asked.

Cissy shook her head.

"Good, because I want a full mass. And I want to
use McGreary on Orchard. Since Nero's son-in-law
took over the business he jacked prices up fifty percent."

"The same type of weapon that killed Eddie shot
Saint-Sault and Lester, too." Nick brought the subject
back to the murders. "The bartender at the Golden
Cue, too." Nick stepped closer, a cop now. "You
knew Otto Chandler, didn't you, Jo Jo?"

"What of it?"

"You knew them all. Who do you think killed
them?"

Jo Jo's hands held no rosary. They merely twisted.
"I told ya I don't know. I'd come from meeting Phil.
The Golden Cue. He liked to meet there. He had a
thing about games. Loved to play them. He stunk at
pool, though. I was trying to teach him." She lapsed
into silence. "I liked Phil. A real gentleman."

"But you were using him, weren't you?" Nick
said.

Jo Jo's face lost its faraway look, turned tough.
"The Lords wanted information."

"And you needed drugs."

Jo Jo's gaze stayed even with Nick's. "Eddie had

driven the Thunderbird into work that day and needed an order picked up, so he gave me the car keys.''

Louisa uttered something in Italian.

''It was early when I left the Golden Cue, so I stashed Eddie's cash under the seat—''

''I found some stuffed in the seat cushions, too,'' Cissy said.

''Maybe sometimes you hid a little there—'' Nick looked at Jo Jo ''—just in case Eddie thought you were skimming again and had Manny frisk you.''

''Like I said, it was early.'' Jo Jo kept her gaze even with Nick's, ignoring his remark. ''So I took a ride over to see Jacques. Somebody at the top must have gotten word that Jacques had been dealing with the Lords, because when I got there, he was dead on the kitchen floor. I heard some noises in the other room. I took off. I don't know if whoever was there saw me or not, but they must have seen Cherry. I drove out to Mama's house, told her what had happened. If the killer only saw the car and mistook Mama for me…we had to get out of there.''

''So you came here?'' Nick said.

''It was Mama's idea. The nuns sent a van, picked us up. And here we are.''

''How did Lester, a civil service clerk from the suburbs, get caught up in an international counterfeiting ring?'' Nick asked.

''Everybody's got their jones. Phil's was gambling. He was into some sharks in a big way and a payment short of losing a limb. He didn't have the money, so he decided to make it. He gave his payment to one of the collectors, who spotted the funny money. The collector takes it to his boss, but instead of turning Phil into fish food, the boss sees a way to expand his business. He offers Phil an opportunity.''

''When did Saint-Sault come in?''

''I'd 'borrowed' some cash from Eddie. Saint-Sault recognized the phony money, tells the guys he works for down south about the operation. They moved in, took over.''

''So Lester kept the accounts and dealt with the big boys?''

''Pissed Jacques off. He'd practically handed them the operation, but the boys at the top knew he fooled around with drugs, didn't trust him. Like I said, Phil was a gentleman and educated. They liked dealing with him.''

''So you sleep with Lester—excuse me, Mrs. Vitelli—'' Nick apologized, ''to get information for the Lords.''

Jo Jo stared at Nick.

''Eventually you found out where the accounts were recorded and who really ran the show, but you were in trouble now. Whoever was at the top knew Eddie and Saint-Sault were working with the Lords, and you were in on it. You call Eddie, tell him to tell the Lords you have everything they need and they can have it for two million.''

''Madonn','' Louisa exclaimed.

''Quite a story.'' Jo Jo neither confirmed nor denied.

Nick rubbed the side of his head. ''I just have one

question. The neighbors, they were shocked when they learned of Lester's death. Said he was such a nice guy, used to print fliers and signs, newsletters for different community organizations. In fact, one of the neighbors—sweet old lady, Cissy here has met her— said that the day Lester died, a nun had visited him that very morning. Come to find out, she visited him within the time frame the autopsy revealed Lester had been shot. So my question is did you get the information you needed before or after you killed Lester?''

Cissy thought about the day she'd followed Eddie and seen a nun on the river walk. ''That was you,'' she said to her sister. ''The other day, by the river. The back brace.'' She stared at Jo Jo. ''The Lords were never going to give you the money. Eddie was trying to hold you off by supplying you with drugs until they could figure out where you were hiding. The drugs were sewn into the back brace.''

Jo Jo look at her sister, her face closed.

''Lester never gave you any information, did he, Jo Jo?'' Nick said. ''It was the other way around. You were giving Lester information. You were the one who told Lester about Saint-Sault and Eddie working with the Lords. That's why the ship was clean on the New Orleans bust. Lester treated you nice. He had manners. Not like Saint-Sault and Big Bill and the rest of the bums.''

Jo Jo's face was expressionless. Her gaze stayed on Nick, challenging him to continue.

''Saint-Sault wasn't dead that night you went to his place. Only when you left. He'd heard the rumors he was going to be blamed for tipping off the southern network about the New Orleans bust, and he planned to say you were the snitch and then become a hero by taking you out.'' Nick paused. ''There was a struggle, you shot him instead. Witnesses see a red 1950s Thunderbird. Now your mother was in danger, too. The two of you come here. The next day, dressed up as a nun, you go to Lester's house. He says he's sorry, real gentlemanly, and then tells you to beat it. You realize he'd been using you like all the others. You panicked. Withdrawal has begun to set in. You'll be damned if you're going to live in a convent the rest of your life. You need cash. You forced Lester to give you information on the operation. When you had what you needed you killed Lester and offered the information to the Lords for two million cash.''

Jo Jo's face stayed defiant, but her hand reached for the Bible beside her on the bench.

Nick pinned her with merciless eyes, his expression inscrutable, his tone matter-of-fact. He was on the job now. ''You called Eddie to set up the deal. You learned your sister's in town and she's driving around in the Thunderbird, a sitting duck. You told Eddie any police, anything happens to Cissy, the deal's off. You get scared for her. Plus you want to score. You went into town, saw Cissy go into the Golden Cue. After she left, you went in to see what she might have learned. Cissy had tipped the bartender with some of the old stuff she'd found in the car seats. Definitely not the quality being produced now. The bartender recognized the funny money, was going to call the cops. If the ring was shut down, the Lords wouldn't need your information. You make something up, tell him you needed assistance and got him out by the Dumpster. After all, you're a nun. And a habit is perfect for hiding a gun.''

Cissy and her mother stared at Jo Jo.

The insolent curve of Jo Jo's lips did not cover the haunted look in her eyes. ''What about Eddie? Why'd I kill him?''

''Better question would be why didn't you kill him? He was an abusive son of a bitch. And you'd told him no cops, but when you picked up the drugs, you spotted the plainclothes who was following Cissy. You think Eddie set you up. You were getting paranoid by now. You could have been made. Eddie might have already put two and two together. You shot him before he could cry 'fore.''

Jo Jo's hands clutched the Bible in her lap.

''Nice work, Detective.'' Tommy Marcus stepped from the bushes, yanked Cissy off the bench and pulled her to him to shield his body. Louisa screamed. A shot rang out, but Nick was forced to aim high to avoid hitting Cissy. Louisa screamed again. Blood flowed from Marcus's shoulder, crimson against the crisp white of his shirt.

''You do the old neighborhood proud, Fiore. Now throw down your weapon.'' Marcus pressed a gun to Cissy's temple.

''You're hit, bleeding, Marcus. You need help. Let her go, and we'll get it for you.''

''You barely grazed me, Fiore. Lucky shot.'' He

pressed the gun harder into Cissy's temple. "Throw down the gun unless you want to see your girlfriend's brains here spoil this peaceful setting."

Nick tossed the gun onto the ground. Marcus moved Cissy to where the gun had landed, kicked it out of reach. The blood oozed from Marcus's shoulder, seeped onto the cream silk of Cissy's blouse.

"You?" Cissy asked. "You ran the counterfeit ring?"

"I try to remain behind the scenes. Unfortunately sometimes I do have to get my hands dirty. Where's the books and the other information you were going to give to the Lords, Jo Jo?"

Jo Jo gripped the Bible.

"Little late for prayers, Jo Jo."

"Shame on you, Tommaso." Louisa spit on the ground. "Your mother turns in her grave right now."

"Shut up, old woman, or you'll be the first to go."

"Go ahead, *bastardo*. Shoot me. This is a beautiful place to die."

"What are you going to do, Tommy? Kill all of us?" Nick asked. The stain of blood was spreading down Marcus's sleeve from his shoulder. "And what about the nuns? What are you going to do? Ask them to pray for your sorry soul?"

Marcus exerted pressure with the gun, tilting Cissy's head. He leaned his mouth to her ear. "Your boyfriend talks big for someone who'll have nothing in thirty years but a pension and the memory of seeing his girl blown away." He flicked his tongue across her earlobe. Nick's expression didn't slip. His gaze stayed cool and murderous.

Jo Jo opened the Bible and snatched a gun from its hollow center. "Let her go." She aimed the gun at Marcus.

He chuckled. "Good God, Jo Jo, you can't even hold the thing steady."

A shot rang out. Nick threw himself forward, taking both Cissy and Marcus down. Another shot sounded. Nick kicked at Marcus's wrist, knocking the gun loose. Marcus rolled for it. Nick hit him with both hands in the lower back, lunged for the gun, slashed it across the side of Marcus's head. Marcus lay facedown in the green grass. His howling stopped. Nick wrenched his arms behind him, handcuffed him, and called for backup. He turned.

Cissy cradled Jo Jo in her lap. She'd ripped off her blouse, pressing it against her little sister's chest to stay the flow of blood, but there was so much blood. Too much blood. Her mother knelt beside them, her hands atop Cissy's, adding pressure. The bloodstain widened, spread, a sea about to swallow her little sister. Cissy stared down at Jo Jo's paling face, saw still the little girl she'd once been.

"I'm sorry, Mama. I'm sorry, Cissy." Jo Jo began to shake in Cissy's arms. "My mistakes."

"S-s-s-h-h." Cissy stroked the hair off her sister's white forehead. "You're going to be fine. Just fine. Help is coming."

The gunshots had brought several nuns running into the garden.

"It's all right, sisters," Nick assured them. "Help is on the way."

"Mama?" Jo Jo asked. She was a child now, trembling and her eyes wide. "Please ask the sisters to come and say a prayer?"

The sisters had already knelt by the girl's wounded body. They began to pray, and Cissy prayed with them.

"It's so cold. I'm so cold," Jo Jo said as the ninety-degree heat beat down on them. Cissy felt the sticky pull of blood soak her palms.

"Hang on, Jo Jo. Hang on," she pleaded. "You're going to be okay."

Jo Jo's body calmed. Her face became peaceful, as if any prayers her little sister had asked for had been answered. Jo Jo closed her eyes.

Cissy clutched her. "Jo Jo! Jo Jo!" She heard the siren in the distance. "Hang on."

As if answering Cissy's prayer, Jo Jo opened her eyes and smiled. Cissy looked down into eyes the same color as hers and smiled back. Her sister's lips moved, but the words were too weak. Cissy bowed her head to hear her.

"The funny part is," Jo Jo whispered, just like the secrets they used to share as children, "I never had anything. No information on the accounts, the organization. I never found it."

Cissy was still holding her when the ambulance arrived. The attendants gently eased her away, lifted Jo Jo's lifeless body onto a gurney, her face to be covered by a sheet once pronounced. The nuns clustered around Cissy and Louisa, comforting them. Cissy looked past them. Nick handed Tommy off to another officer, his gaze on her. She broke away from the women, walked toward him. He met her halfway.

She looked down at Jo Jo's gun he had recovered. "A .22?"

He nodded.

She looked away, watched Tommy being led out of the garden. "You finally got to use those cuffs." Her voice shook.

He wrapped his arms around her, and she wept.

Chapter Seventeen

The newly-dug dirt smelled rich, fertile, like life.

"We should join the others back at the house," Nick said softly.

Cissy stared at the turned earth, the sprays of flowers. "Yes." But she did not move. She did not cry. Nothing. There was nothing. Nick put his arm around her shoulders. There was Nick. She leaned on him. She had learned to lean this past week.

Attempted murder charges had been filed against Marcus, but with the bills Cissy had found in the Thunderbird the only evidence, no witnesses coming forth and Marcus not giving up a thing, it was unlikely any indictments on counterfeiting charges could be filed. For Nick, it was a case of the bar bombing all over again. The police knew the crime, knew the criminal, but without solid evidence, no convictions.

Cissy was staying with her mother. She'd moved out of Nick's place as soon as they'd found Louisa, but had still been subjected to a daily 'they-don't-buy-the-cow-if-they-can-get-the-milk-free' maternal diatribe. She didn't bother to explain that she and Nick weren't the cow-buying types. Their mating was free milk and fine.

Louisa was selling the business and the house and moving to a golf cart community in Boca Raton to make a fresh start. Cissy had gone with her to the bar to meet the real estate agent and spied Gentleman George on the corner. Staying true to her resolutions, she'd gone over to give him a few bills. When she'd gotten up close, she'd noticed the toupee cockeyed on his head. She'd given him twenty dollars for it, checking to make sure the bill was legit. When she found a key inside the hairpiece's hem—a key identical to the safety deposit box key she had from First Trust—she said another of the prayers that were becoming much more frequent lately. A court order was issued and the box opened, but it was empty except for the deed to a cemetery plot. Phil really had loved playing games. With the Lords closing in and Marcus getting tense, Lester must have been getting nervous. He needed an insurance policy to prevent any harm coming to him. He must have hidden information on the operation, but where? Some place where he could get at it if necessary but others could not—especially if something happened to him and his mother's financial well-being became suspect, possibly even confiscated should it be determined the money was ill-gotten gains.

"We should go," Nick reminded again gently.

They headed toward Cherry. Pauline had driven her mother back to the house with the others. The Thunderbird had become like an old friend to Cissy.

"When are you going back to New York?" Nick asked.

It was the first time either of them had brought up the subject of Cissy's leaving.

"I don't know."

"Does your job expect you back soon?"

Time to come clean. "Actually I'm in between careers at the moment." Close enough.

Nick glanced at her. "You quit your job?"

"Company went under. I wouldn't have lasted much longer anyway. I was a lousy stockbroker."

"What are you going to do?"

"I'm exploring several options."

"Haven't a clue, have you?"

She smiled for the first time in several days. Past Nick's shoulder she saw a woman tending to a potted geranium in front of a gravestone. It was Mrs. Lester. Her caretaker stood nearby. Cissy had seen the signs announcing that the bingo hall on Armory would soon be under new management. Lester's Lucky Palace Coming Soon. Phil would have liked that, Cissy thought.

"There's Mrs. Lester."

Nick looked in the direction Cissy indicated.

"I'm going to say hello," Cissy told him.

The couple walked toward the old woman kneeling before her son's grave. Another headstone stood next to Phil's, two brothers buried beside each other. Cissy looked down at the woman's stooped back.

"Mrs. Lester, it's me, Cissy Spagnola. How are you?"

The woman squinted up at them. "You're dating the cop?"

Nick glanced at Cissy. "We've had several conversations the last few days," Nick explained. He took the woman's elbow as she got up, and steadied her. "How are you, Mrs. Lester?"

The woman shaded her eyes. "I keep waiting to be manhandled."

Cissy swallowed a grin. "I see you got your bingo hall."

"Grand opening in a month. You and lover boy come on in. I'll give you a couple cards on the house."

"Thank you. I'll do that."

She eyed Nick. "And don't be sending no patrols for a shakedown. I run a clean establishment."

"Yes, ma'am."

The old woman looked at the graves, her face suddenly older and wistful.

"Beautiful stones," Cissy commented.

"When Phil's brother died, Phil designed the headstone himself, had it custom made. About a month ago he had his own…" The woman stared at her children's graves. "Let's go," she said, turning to her companion. "I've got to pee."

The woman tottered off with her caretaker. Cissy stared down at the marker. "One look inside Lester's medicine cabinet and you knew he was organized, but designing your own gravestone, that goes beyond anal."

"Lester knew things were heating up, that his luck,

which had let him down in the past, would run out again.''

''I suppose.'' She studied the marker. ''Where's the evidence, Phil? What'd you do with it?''

''Afraid that answer went with Lester to the grave. Come on.'' Nick gently turned Cissy away.

They were almost to the car when Cissy stopped, released a laugh.

Nick looked at her with concern.

''He took it to his grave. He took it with him to his grave.''

''Are you okay?''

''All right, Lester was a little on the retentive side, but maybe he had another reason for having his gravestone made?''

''Such as?''

''Lester wanted to hide the evidence, right? Hide it where he could get to it, but should something happen to him, others would never find it.''

Nick smiled. ''I'll call the manufacturer tomorrow, see if Phil's special design included any special features.''

''Hide-and-seek.'' Cissy's smile slipped into sadness. ''Jo Jo loved that game when we were little.''

Nick put his arm around her. They started toward the car again.

''This detective work isn't too hard. Maybe I'll just hang out a shingle, open up my own private investigation agency.''

''Here?''

Cissy slanted a glance at him. "I don't know. Maybe. Maybe not. I was kidding, really."

They walked a little farther.

"Or maybe I wasn't," she said.

"Cissy?"

"Yeah?"

"Stay."

She stopped short, stared at him. She didn't expect more. She hadn't even expected this.

His fingers hooked inside her belt loops, pulled her to him. "Stay."

She studied his face. "Damn." She had to turn away, not wanting him to see how much she wanted to say yes. He curved his hand to her cheek, turned her toward him.

"Damn." But she was smiling now. Hell, she never could say no to a dare.

He lowered his mouth to hers. They came together. The way she liked it. The way he liked it. Simple.

Yeah, right.

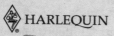
HARLEQUIN

INTRIGUE®

COMING NEXT MONTH

#741 A WARRIOR'S MISSION by Rita Herron
Colorado Confidential

When Colorado Confidential agent Night Walker arrived to investigate the Langworthy baby kidnapping, he discovered that the baby was *his*. A night of passion with Holly Langworthy months ago had left him a father, and now it was up to him to find his son—and win the heart of the woman he'd never forgotten.

#742 THE THIRD TWIN by Dani Sinclair
Heartskeep

Alexis Ryder's life was turned upside down the day she came home to find her father murdered, a briefcase full of money and a note revealing she was illegally adopted. Desperate to learn the truth, she had no choice but to team up with charming police officer Wyatt Crossley—the only man who seemed to have the answers she was seeking.

#743 UNDER SURVEILLANCE by Gayle Wilson
Phoenix Brotherhood

Phoenix Brotherhood operative John Edmonds was given one last case to prove himself to the agency: keep an eye on Kelly Lockett, the beautiful heir to her family's charitable foundation. But their mutual attraction was threatening his job—and might put her life in danger....

#744 MOUNTAIN SHERIFF by B.J. Daniels
Cascades Concealed

Journalist Charity Jenkins had been pursuing sexy sheriff Mitch Tanner since they were children. Trouble was, the man was a confirmed bachelor. But when strange things started happening to Charity and Mitch realized she might be in danger, he knew he had to protect her. Would he also find love where he least expected it?

#745 BOYS IN BLUE by Rebecca York (Ruth Glick writing as Rebecca York), Ann Voss Peterson and Patricia Rosemoor
Bachelors At Large

Three brothers' lives were changed forever when one of their own was arrested for murder. Now they had to unite to prove his innocence and discover the real killer...but they never thought they'd find *love*, as well!

#746 FOR THE SAKE OF THEIR BABY by Alice Sharpe

When her uncle's dead body was found in his mansion, Liz Chase's husband, Alex, took the rap for what he thought was a deliberate murder by his pregnant wife. But once he was released from prison, and discovered that his loving wife hadn't committed the crime, could they work together to find the *real* killer... and rekindle their relationship?

Visit us at www.eHarlequin.com

HICNM1103

HARLEQUIN®
INTRIGUE®

has a new lineup of books to keep you on
the edge of your seat throughout the winter.
So be on the alert for...

BACHELORS AT LARGE

**Bold and brash—these men have sworn to serve
and protect as officers of the law...and only the
most special women can "catch" these good guys!**

UNDER HIS PROTECTION
BY AMY J. FETZER
(October 2003)

UNMARKED MAN
BY DARLENE SCALERA
(November 2003)

BOYS IN BLUE
A special 3-in-1 volume with
REBECCA YORK (Ruth Glick writing as Rebecca York),
ANN VOSS PETERSON AND PATRICIA ROSEMOOR
(December 2003)

CONCEALED WEAPON
BY SUSAN PETERSON
(January 2004)

GUARDIAN OF HER HEART
BY LINDA O. JOHNSTON
(February 2004)

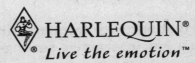

HARLEQUIN®
Live the emotion™

**Visit us at www.eHarlequin.com
and www.tryintrigue.com**

HIBBONTS

eHARLEQUIN.com

Your favorite authors are just a click away
at www.eHarlequin.com!

- Take our **Sister Author Quiz** and
  we'll match you up with the author
  most like you!

- Choose from over 500
  author **profiles!**

- Chat with your favorite authors
  on our **message boards.**

- Are you an author in the making?
  Get advice from published authors
  in **The Inside Scoop!**

- Get the latest on **author appearances**
  and tours!

*Want to know more about your
favorite romance authors?*

Choose from over 500 author profiles!

**Learn about your favorite authors
in a fun, interactive setting—
visit www.eHarlequin.com today!**

INTAUTH

If you enjoyed what you just read,
then we've got an offer you can't resist!

Take 2 bestselling
love stories FREE!
Plus get a FREE surprise gift!

Clip this page and mail it to Harlequin Reader Service

IN U.S.A.	IN CANADA
3010 Walden Ave.	P.O. Box 609
P.O. Box 1867	Fort Erie, Ontario
Buffalo, N.Y. 14240-1867	L2A 5X3

YES! Please send me 2 free Harlequin Intrigue® novels and my free surprise gift. After receiving them, if I don't wish to receive anymore, I can return the shipping statement marked cancel. If I don't cancel, I will receive 6 brand-new novels each month, before they're available in stores! In the U.S.A., bill me at the bargain price of $3.99 plus 25¢ shipping and handling per book and applicable sales tax, if any*. In Canada, bill me at the bargain price of $4.74 plus 25¢ shipping and handling per book and applicable taxes**. That's the complete price and a savings of at least 10% off the cover prices—what a great deal! I understand that accepting the 2 free books and gift places me under no obligation ever to buy any books. I can always return a shipment and cancel at any time. Even if I never buy another book from Harlequin, the 2 free books and gift are mine to keep forever.

182 HDN DU9K
382 HDN DU9L

Name	(PLEASE PRINT)	
Address	Apt.#	
City	State/Prov.	Zip/Postal Code

* Terms and prices subject to change without notice. Sales tax applicable in N.Y.
** Canadian residents will be charged applicable provincial taxes and GST.
    All orders subject to approval. Offer limited to one per household and not valid to
    current Harlequin Intrigue® subscribers.
    ® are registered trademarks of Harlequin Enterprises Limited.

INT03

New York Times bestselling author
DEBBIE MACOMBER

brings you a brand-new and long-awaited book
featuring three of her most popular characters—
the matchmaking and always mischievous
angels Shirley, Goodness and Mercy.
And she brings it to Superromance!

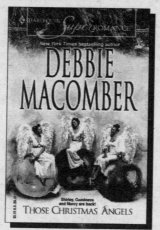

THOSE CHRISTMAS ANGELS

Available in November,
wherever Harlequin books are sold.

Visit us at www.eHarlequin.com

HSRTCADM

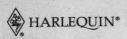

HARLEQUIN®

INTRIGUE®

Nestled deep in the Cascade Mountains of Oregon, the close-knit community of Timber Falls is visited by evil. Could one of their own be lurking in the shadows…?

CASCADES CONCEALED

B.J. Daniels

takes you on a journey to the remote Northwest in a new series of books far removed from the fancy big city. Here, folks are down-to-earth, but some have a tendency toward trouble when the rainy season comes…and it's about to start pouring!

Look for

MOUNTAIN SHERIFF
December 2003

and

DAY OF RECKONING
March 2004

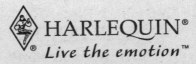

HARLEQUIN®
Live the emotion™

Visit us at www.eHarlequin.com

HICQMS

HARLEQUIN®
INTRIGUE®

Our unique brand of high-caliber romantic
suspense just cannot be contained. And to meet
our readers' demands, Harlequin Intrigue is
expanding its publishing lineup
to include **SIX** breathtaking titles
every month!

Here's what we have
in store for you:

❑ A trilogy of **Heartskeep** stories
by Dani Sinclair

❑ More great **Bachelors at Large** books
featuring sexy, single cops

❑ Plus outstanding contributions from your
favorite Harlequin Intrigue authors, such as
Amanda Stevens, B.J. Daniels and Gayle Wilson

MORE variety.
MORE pulse-pounding excitement.
MORE of your favorite authors and series.
Every month.

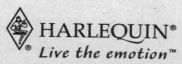

HARLEQUIN®
Live the emotion™

Visit us at www.tryIntrigue.com

HI4T06B